THE BALFOUR BRIDES

A p...

Scandal ha...

Its glittering, ... are in disgrace.

Banished from ... Balfour mansion, they're sent to the boldest, most magnificent men in the world to be wedded, bedded…and tamed!

And so begins a scandalous saga of dazzling glamour and passionate surrender.

**Each month, Harlequin Presents®
is delighted to bring you an exciting new
installment from THE BALFOUR BRIDES.
You won't want to miss out!**

Eight volumes to collect and treasure!

"You have led a very sheltered life, Sophie Balfour."

Part of Marco had clung to the belief that the wholesome innocence thing was part of an act, but nobody, he realized now, was that good an actress.

As he watched, she reached out and touched the bed with her hand, in doing so turning a little so that she presented her profile rather than her back to him. At some point since they had parted she had gathered her hair into a haphazard knot, dragging it from her face and revealing a profile that was classically pure.

But it was not her face that Marco's eyes were glued to, it was her body, for her hair was not the only change. The mushroom-colored shirt that had enveloped her diminutive frame from shoulder to knee was gone.

The jeans underneath were utilitarian and ill fitting—no surprise there. The surprise was that Sophie Balfour had a waist, and one that he could have spanned with his hands.

Had Marco felt inclined to mix business with pleasure it would be a pleasure to explore that body, because if the waist had been a shock the rest of her was a total and utter jaw-dropping revelation.

Kim Lawrence

SOPHIE AND THE SCORCHING SICILIAN

The Balfour Brides

HARLEQUIN®

TORONTO • NEW YORK • LONDON
AMSTERDAM • PARIS • SYDNEY • HAMBURG
STOCKHOLM • ATHENS • TOKYO • MILAN • MADRID
PRAGUE • WARSAW • BUDAPEST • AUCKLAND

Special thanks and acknowledgment are given to
Kim Lawrence for her contribution to
The Balfour Brides series.

Recycling programs
for this product may
not exist in your area.

ISBN-13: 978-0-373-12952-2

SOPHIE AND THE SCORCHING SICILIAN

First North American Publication 2010.

All about the author...
Kim Lawrence

KIM LAWRENCE comes from English/Irish stock. Though lacking much authentic Welsh blood, she was born and brought up in north Wales. She returned there when she married, and her sons were both born on Anglesey, an island off the coast. Though not isolated, Anglesey is a little off the beaten track, but lively Dublin, which Kim loves, is only a short ferry ride away.

Today they live on the farm her husband was brought up on. Welsh is the first language of many people in this area and Kim's husband and sons are all bilingual—she is having a lot of fun, not to mention a few headaches, trying to learn the language!

With small children, the unsocial hours of nursing didn't look attractive, so—encouraged by a husband who thinks she can do anything she sets her mind to—Kim tried her hand at writing. Always a keen Harlequin reader, it seemed natural for her to write a romance novel. Now she can't imagine doing anything else.

She is a keen gardener and cook and enjoys running—often on the beach, as on an island the sea is never very far away. She is usually accompanied by her Jack Russell, Sprout— don't ask, it's a long story!

To my two boys who have grown into
rather splendid young men

CHAPTER ONE

SOPHIE paused at the top of the steps and consulted her notebook. She turned to the pencilled map drawn in her own neat hand before glancing up to double-check the number on the door of the modest Georgian terrace. It was in a street filled with rows of similar houses, but then, as they always said, when it came to property it was all about location.

She shaded her eyes from the July sun as she directed her gaze towards the luxury cars parked along the tree-lined street. They seemed to suggest that, in estate-agent speak, this location could be classed as highly desirable.

She turned her attention back to the building. This was, she decided, definitely the place, though a further search revealed there was nothing as vulgar as a sign to identify it on the door.

Small but exclusive, her father had said, with a growing reputation for excellence. Exactly the sort of place, he had assured Sophie, for her to spread her artistic wings.

'A springboard for future success!' he had enthused. 'You could go places with your talent, Sophie, you just need to get out there and show the world what you can do!'

So, no pressure, then.

Sophie had resisted the temptation to point out that a home-study course in interior decorating didn't necessarily qualify her to achieve world domination in the field of interior design, not overnight anyway.

There would be no interview, it seemed, and when she had asked when she started the new job, her father's reply had tipped her over into outright panic.

'Monday…this Monday…do you think I can?'

Her father had looked *stern* and Oscar Balfour could look *very* stern, but not normally with her.

She had never given him cause; she had always towed the line, and there had never been any major dramas in her life. She'd never needed rescuing, or been the subject of embarrassing headlines; there were no unsuitable men in her past…she was an open and fairly boring book.

Depressing when you thought about it.

'I *know* you can.'

'You do?'

'I know, Sophie, that you and your sisters will not disappoint me. I have faith in you. Your sisters have all accepted a challenge.'

And if she didn't what did that make her?

'I know they have.' And she missed them.

'This is my fault,' Oscar Balfour had insisted.

Sophie's kind heart had ached to see the father she loved hold himself personally responsible and she'd said warmly, though not entirely truthfully, 'You've been a wonderful father.'

As she hugged him she'd seen the tabloid open on his desk. Knowing it contained a particularly vicious editorial, she'd heard herself say, 'I'll do it.'

Sophie had left the room with an emotional lump the size of a golf ball in her throat, in a state of shock but determined not to let down her father and sisters; for once in her life she would act like a Balfour.

A week later and the lump was still there, but as she lifted a hand to knock tentatively on the half-open door it had been joined by a tight knot of anxiety lying like a leaden weight in her stomach.

She still felt in shock.

She knew none of this should have come as a surprise. Since the drama of the scandalous events surrounding the annual Balfour Charity Ball, she had watched as one by one her sisters had been sent away to prove themselves in the world without the cushion of the Balfour wealth and influence.

But time had passed and Sophie had waited nervously for her invitation to her father's study, and when it hadn't materialised she had relaxed a little, assuming she was safe—then...it came.

The sympathetic look she received from her father's butler as she let herself in by a side door to the manor had made her wonder, but the tearful hug from the cook had confirmed it— she had not been overlooked.

Her father had, he said, taken his time to find the perfect position for her. Sophie, who knew that her perfect position was at home at the Balfour gatehouse with her mother, had tried to sound suitably appreciative of his efforts.

Sophie glanced at her watch; she was fifteen minutes early for her first day. Wondering if that made her appear eager or desperate she toyed with the idea of taking a walk and coming back later.

No, it was now or never—don't be a wimp, Sophie, you can do this! Taking a deep breath she was looking around for the bell when she caught the door with her elbow and it swung inwards.

'Hello!'

There was no reply.

Taking her courage by the scruff of its neck she stepped through the open door. The room she stepped into was laid out like a country house drawing room, the decor aimed at people who had as much money as taste.

The aroma of coffee was her first impression; the second was the lovely and clever use of texture and colour in the soft furnishing. It was clearly a showroom of sorts, though there were no price tags on either the beautifully displayed individual pieces of modern art or the equally fine antique items.

Sophie was both impressed and daunted, as this was a far cry from her little work room at the Balfour gatehouse with her drawing board, colour charts and wallpaper samples.

She brushed her fingertips along a beautiful vibrant-coloured kilim that had been draped over a leather chesterfield and struggled to see herself working here.

'Hello?' she called out again.

She was standing there feeling like a spare part and wondering what to do next when she heard the sound of voices; the noise was coming from the far end of the room, but she couldn't see anyone. With a puzzled frown drawing her feathery brows into a straight line, she moved towards the sound of the voices when she realised that what she had assumed was a wall was actually a portable screen.

The voices were the other side and as she aproached they got louder.

She peered through a gap in the screen and saw another area laid out beyond, lit by a pair of stunning chandeliers. This time the style was strongly Gustavian; pale and deceptively simple, the light airy feel was further enhanced by a stunning antique mirror in an ornate carved white-painted frame that took centre stage.

The building was clearly a great deal larger than it looked from the outside.

She opened her mouth to speak, caught the word *Balfour*, and closed it again, revealing herself now might cause embarrassment to the people on the other side of the screen. Two women, by the sound of their voices, though all Sophie could see were the tops of their heads above the high back of a wooden bench.

She was about to move to the opposite side of the room when she heard the person who hadn't yet spoken exclaim, 'One of the Balfour girls—you've got to be kidding! Work here! Do they work? And risk breaking a nail, surely not.'

'Miaow…if you were a society heiress to a fortune, would you work, darling?'

'Let me see…'

Sophie heard both girls laugh.

'But you'd have to share the fortune with…how many sisters are there?'

'Are we including the one they've just discovered?'

Normally a pretty placid person Sophie felt her face flush with anger at this mocking reference—anger she felt on behalf of her half-sister Mia, who was the result of an affair their father had many years ago.

Oscar had welcomed the daughter he hadn't known about into the family and despite the fact she hadn't known her for long Sophie felt a special closeness to her beautiful half-Italian sister.

'And then Zoe Balfour isn't really a Balfour at all…maybe she's the one that's coming here?' one of the voices speculated.

There was a certain malicious amusement in the voice that responded. 'Yeah, maybe Daddy's cut her off now he knows she's not his. I do wish I could have been a fly on the wall at the 100th Balfour Charity Ball!'

Sophie's hands clenched into fists at her side as she bit her tongue, longing to set the record straight, but she was hampered by the fact that she couldn't, without revealing that she'd been eavesdropping.

Sure Zoe had been outed as illegitimate at the Balfour Ball and the ensuing scandal had caused their father's serious overhaul of his parental style but as far as he and all of them were concerned Zoe was a Balfour no matter what her genetic parentage was.

'So how many are there?'

'Six, seven, who knows…but what wouldn't I give to have their looks and money!' came the wistful response.

Eight, thought Sophie, silently amending their total, and she seconded their wish, at least for the looks part anyway. The money part had never been a problem for her in that she didn't have expensive tastes, but what the Balfour name gave her was the luxury of following her instincts.

And Sophie's instincts drew her like a homing pigeon back to Balfour, where her mother lived in the gatehouse since the tragic death of her second husband. Sophie's eyes misted as her thoughts touched on the man who had been a second father to his wife's three daughters.

For a short time Sri Lanka had been home for Sophie but now the Balfour estate in Buckinghamshire was the one place she really felt she belonged, it was the place where there was no pressure to be something she wasn't.

Unlike her sisters, she wasn't an instantly recognisable face except to the people who worked on the Balfour estate and the locals in the village.

'I have never provided you girls with challenges,' Oscar Balfour had lamented. 'Children need to be pushed, but it is never too late. I have been a negligent father, but I mean to make amends. *Independence*, Sophie,' he'd said, indicating the rule that she would find most valuable, though he warned it would not be easy for her to learn. 'A member of the Balfour family must strive to develop themselves and not rely on the family name to get them through life.'

'Which ever one it is you can be sure that we'll end up stuck with her work and ours.'

Listening to the grunt of assent from the second girl Sophie gritted her teeth and thought she'd show them that this Balfour was not just a pretty face—actually, not a pretty face at all, but that she couldn't do anything about.

However, she did have a work ethic and she would show them that she wasn't afraid of hard work.

'What was Amber thinking, taking her on?'

Sophie, unashamedly eavesdropping now, strained to hear as the other girl lowered her voice to a confidential undertone.

'You know that diamond bracelet that Amber wears…?'

There was a pause when presumably the other girl had nodded. 'Well, that was a little parting gift from Oscar Balfour.'

'Amber and Oscar Balfour…wow! Why didn't I know that?'

'It was years ago, and it didn't last long.'

'Oscar Balfour…he's quite attractive for an older man, isn't he? Actually, quite sexy and he looks like he knows…'

Grimacing, Sophie had no desire to hear the women discussing her father in *that* sort of detail and covered her ears. When she uncovered them again one girl was saying, 'And let's face it—a Balfour girl working here… God, you couldn't *pay* for that sort of advertising.'

'That twin…Bella, the skinny one…?'

'The impossibly gorgeous one?'

'All right, the gorgeous one. Do you remember that time she was pictured wearing a dress from that charity shop and the shelves emptied overnight.'

Sophie did remember. She remembered when the subject had been raised during a family dinner.

Zoe had joked that she didn't know what all the fuss was about. Sophie, she said, had been wearing charity-shop clothes for years.

Sophie had joined in the laughter, even inviting further hilarity by comparing the practicality and comfort of the sports bras she favoured with push ups that consisted of a few scraps of lace. But later in her own room she had looked at her wardrobe, filled with the sorts of clothes—or tents in boring colours, as Annie had once described her style—that made her glamorous sisters despair, and she hadn't smiled.

The tent situation was not accidental, but her taller, slimmer sisters who did not have breasts that made men snigger and stare would not have understand her decision to hide her ample bosom under voluminous tops.

In a family famed for beauty, grace and wit—the very things that Sophie had missed out on—she had, presumably by way of compensation, been given instead the clumsy gene. A nuisance…yes, but to Sophie's way of thinking not as much of a blight as having heads turn when you walked into a room the way they did automatically for her sisters.

A Balfour girl who disliked the limelight—a *Balfour girl*…how she hated that phrase—who was not witty or beautiful, made her something of a freak.

So much so that Sophie sometimes wondered if the real Balfour baby had been left at the hospital the day they brought her home—but she had the Balfour blue eyes, the same piercing Balfour blue of her father's eyes.

For the average Balfour, being the centre of attention was as commonplace as breathing and something that they took as much for granted.

It was Sophie's idea of hell.

But she had a solution. It had taken her time but at twenty-three she had just about perfected the art of fading into the background. Being short and on the dumpy side gave her a head start, so now the only time strangers noticed her was when she managed to trip over her own feet, or spill something.

She did both in graceful unison when a voice behind her said, 'Can I help you?'

Sophie yelped, spun around and dropped her bag on the waxed floorboards. A tall blonde woman dressed in a snug-fitting red sheath that showed off her slim figure watched, one brow raised, as Sophie dropped to her knees and began to pick up the coins that had tipped out of her purse.

'Sorry…I…' Pushing her hair back from her flushed face Sophie held out her hand.

The woman looked at it with a lack of enthusiasm.

Sophie dropped her arm. 'I'm Sophie…Sophie Balfour—I'm meant to be here…working… I… My father…'

'*You* are Sophie Balfour?' The blonde woman looked openly sceptical.

Sophie who had encountered this response before nodded and repressed the impulse to say, *No, I'm an impostor! I kid-*

napped the real Sophie Balfour! 'Yes. I think you were expecting me.'

'I was expecting…'

The woman didn't finish the sentence; she didn't need to. It was no struggle to fill in the blanks—she'd been expecting someone with glamour and style.

And she got me.

The blonde compressed her red-painted lips. If there had been any movement possible in her forehead—Sophie had seen more lines on a newborn baby than on this woman's smooth face—she would definitely have been frowning, but she made a quick recovery and produced a strained smile.

'I'm Amber Charles. Your father tells me you're very talented.'

Sophie gave a self-deprecating shrug, but there was animation in her expression as she admitted, 'I enjoy colour and texture…' She stopped, the animation fading when she realised that the svelte designer was regarding the colour and texture of her outfit with a look of growing horror.

She glanced down, genuinely not sure what she was wearing.

'I've got my CV.' Her school grades would not put an admiring light in the other woman's eyes.

Sophie had shown no talent for anything academic, or for that matter anything sporting at Westfields, and she had often wished she'd had the guts to run away from the place like Kat. But instead she had kept a low profile and waited for the day she could leave.

Amber held up a hand and shook her head. 'I'm sure they're excellent.'

Want to bet? Sophie thought, and smiled.

'A high level of girls from Westfields go to Oxbridge. My cousin's daughter graduates next summer—she adores it. Which university did you attend?'

'Actually, I didn't go to university.'

The pencilled brows lifted.

'I did a home-study course,' she explained, wondering if she ought to say she passed with flying colours.

'How…nice.'

Sophie watched her boss struggle to smile; clearly her dad had been economic with the details when he wangled her a job with his ex-flame.

'Well, Sophie, what are we going to do with you?'

From her expression Sophie was thinking it possible that *vanish* was her first choice.

'You may be talented…'

Sophie knew she ought to rush into this doubtful pause and confidently announce she was actually not just talented but a bit of a genius, but selling herself was not her thing.

'…but it's not enough to have talent…'

'It isn't?'

'Of course not, this is a very competitive market and we have to do everything. Appearances, I'm afraid, are equally impor- tant. Our clients expect a certain… You know, I think you'd be happier working behind the scenes.'

'So you want me to work behind the scenes?'

Sophie, who knew this translated as *I can't risk having a client see you*, was not offended; this was the best news she had had all day.

Unbending slightly as it became clear Sophie was not going to be difficult, Amber inclined her head in assent. 'You know, my dear, you should smile more often. It makes you look almost pretty.'

CHAPTER TWO

MARCO left his car and walked the last mile up the winding driveway that led to the palazzo that had been in his family for centuries.

In his pocket he carried the heavy key to the massive front door that he had locked a year ago.

Locked and walked away from without a backward glance. At the time he had told himself the gesture was symbolic; he had been locking the door on his mistakes, his humiliation, his broken marriage.

He had told himself that it was about moving forward, leaving the past behind and getting on with his life. It was logical to channel his energies, to streamline. *Streamlining*, he mused with a contemptuous grimace, had a much more palatable ring to it than *running away*.

His strategy might have been based on self-delusion but his goal had been financial gain and it had worked.

Cutting himself off from the multitude of society social events that he had always believed his duty to attend, as guardian of the ancient name of Speranza, had left him with more time to devote to new business ventures—and they had been successful beyond the most wildly optimistic predictions.

No longer required by a moral code—outdated but genetically imprinted—to respect his marriage vows even while his wife had flaunted her infidelities, Marco had found time to date, though *date* perhaps implied an intimacy that went beyond the bedroom, and his liaisons with a series of attractive women had not.

If he was aware of a certain post-coital emptiness Marco felt no desire to fill the void with any emotional complications. Emptiness was a lot easier to live with than romantic involvement, and not being the certifiably insane romantic he had been when he had married Allegra, there was no way he was about to hand some woman his heart so that she could stomp on it with her delicate heels.

No, *that* part of his new life was no mistake, but running away from his responsibilities had been; he could see that now. He owed a duty to his name and the people who served his family, some for generations. He was ashamed of the selfish and cowardly impulse that had made him turn his back on them just because he didn't want the constant reminders of his failure.

His jaw firmed as his keen gaze swept the scene ahead. Others should not suffer for his failings. The duty that was as much an integral part of Marco's genetic make-up as the colour of his eyes had brought him back today—duty and a desire to regain something he had…*lost*?

Could a man know he had lost something and be unable to name it? Marco, not inclined towards such philosophical debate, had no idea but he did know that his pulse rate did not quicken with anticipation as he approached his home as it once had; he recognised the familiar sights and smells but he did not *feel* them as he once had.

He had always been passionately proud of his inheritance. When had that passion become duty? he wondered as he paused and looked down at his ancestral home.

The home he had brought his bride to, the home he had walked away from the day she ran off with his best friend and he had filed for divorce.

He pushed away the black thoughts from a year ago—in the

history of this ancient building it was a blink of an eye; in his life more than enough time to lick his wounds as any longer would smack of self-indulgence. His pride had been injured, but a man did not regain self-respect by running away, and any bad memories these walls held for him now would be easier to live with than Allegra had been!

The marriage had been a disaster from the start, but it wasn't her drinking and infidelity that had sickened him most; it had been the fact he had fallen for her sweet innocent act.

And there were other memories here.

This was where he had spent his childhood.

He had roamed the estate and enjoyed a degree of freedom that he might not have had his parents been more hands-on.

But his actress mother was often away on location. His father, a distant figure, had been around more frequently, but having left a promising law career to enter politics, where his integrity made him as many enemies as allies, his family came a very poor second to being a public crusading figure.

Perhaps one more enemy, Marco thought, his eyes growing bleak as he recalled the grim day in the nineties when he had learnt from a news broadcast that there had been an assassination.

One bullet—his father had died instantly and the title had come to Marco.

'Marchese.'

Marco was startled from his dark reflections by the form of address he did not use in his professional life.

'Alberto!' A smile of genuine pleasure tugged his mobile mouth into an upward curve that softened the austerity of his classically cut features as he moved forward, his hand out-stretched in welcome.

The other man jumped out of the open-topped vehicle with an agility that many men twenty years his junior would have envied and came to shake his hand.

'You are looking well, Alberto,' Marco approved truthfully.

'As are you.'

He clapped the younger man on the shoulder and felt the hard muscles under his fingers.

The younger man's expensive suit did not hide a soft belly; it hid a body that was hard and tough from riding and from indulging in the sort of extreme sports that Alberto did not totally approve of.

He was relieved to see that the city life of high finance—a man should not spend his days indoors—had not softened Marco Speranza, but sorry that there was a hardness and cynicism in his green eyes that had not been there in his youth.

But then a man who had been through what he had was allowed a little cynicism.

'You are keeping an eye on the new man?'

The estate manager Marco had taken on had been in the post for three years now but to Alberto, whose family had served Marco's for generations, the younger man would always be *new*.

'He is a hard worker.'

Marco grinned. 'Praise indeed coming from you, Alberto, and how is Natalia?' Marco's voice softened as he said the name.

In her official capacity as cook Alberto's wife had ruled the kitchen when Marco had been growing up; in her unofficial capacity she had been the person who had comforted him on the occasions when a mother would normally have offered hugs.

Even when his own mother had been around, she did not do hugs except when there was a camera to record the moment of maternal devotion.

'She is well, *Marchese*.' Alberto angled a questioning look up at the tall man. 'And she would like to see you…?'

Marco heard the question and felt a fresh stab of guilt. He had neglected many things, including old friends, when he had cut himself off in the scandalous aftermath of the divorce.

'And she will,' he promised. 'But not today, I'm afraid.' He flicked his cuff and glanced at his watch, mentally calculating how long the journey back to Palermo would take him. 'I have a meeting in Naples.'

'You have been missed.'

Aware of the reproach in the other man's voice Marco nodded; he felt he deserved it. For a while the palazzo had been a battleground, and involved in the bitter war of attrition he had forgotten it was also his home.

Marco admitted this with a humility that would have made his business competitors stare. 'I was wrong to stay away. I have missed being here, so I'm here today to see what needs doing.'

'You are coming home?'

What sort of home? Marco struggled to maintain his positive expression as his eyes lifted to the Renaissance facade. Fortunately no major structural work needed to be done, he told himself, concentrating on the fabric of the building, not on the dark emotions he experienced when he looked at his ancestral home.

Would he ever be able to wipe away the shadows left by his failed marriage? Would he ever be able to look at this building and think of it as a home in the true sense of the word? It would take more than a fresh coat of paint, though being a pragmatic man he thought that would be a start.

'Yes, but first I want to make it…habitable.'

Alberto nodded in total understanding. Too much understanding, for Marco's liking; pity, even from an old friend, was not something he enjoyed.

'I just need to find someone who understands what this building deserves.'

Someone who felt as he did about preserving its integrity; someone capable of feeling passionate about their work…*to compensate for his own lack of it*… He tore his eyes away from the facade and said, 'And of course a new housekeeper—do you think Natalia would consider it?'

During one of his absences Allegra had ousted Natalia from her kitchen and replaced her with a French chef. On his return

Marco had sacked the chef and tried to persuade Natalia to return, but she had steadfastly refused to enter the palazzo while Allegra was mistress there.

Allegra had retaliated for his actions by getting drunk in public and being photographed half naked in the back of a cab with a boy who worked in the nightclub she had just fallen out of at four in the morning.

So it had been a win–win situation.

Alberto beamed, and said, 'I think it might be possible…'

Marco pulled the key from his pocket, inhaled and approached the door.

His instructions had been that the place was not to be touched and they had been followed to the letter; barring the dust, it was all just as it had been.

A walk through the building did not lift his mood. In his youth this had been a showplace; now the whole building had a pervading air of gloom and neglect that the grandeur of the architecture and furnishing could not hide.

Had it always been this dark and depressing? he wondered as he pulled aside a dusty drape to let in some light. The light revealed damp patches on the high, carved ceiling and this fresh physical evidence of his neglect deepened the frown on his wide brow.

He cursed softly under his breath, and as he strode purposefully out into the sunlight and the waiting Alberto, Marco determined to bring light and life back into his home.

'All I need is to find someone I trust, who appreciates what this building deserves.'

It had not seemed a major problem to find such a person when he'd said it, but a week later, and after six pitches by possible candidates that had left him totally unmoved, Marco was realising he might have to cast his net wider.

Recalling a comment by someone who had spent last

summer in London concerning a firm they had used to refurbish their penthouse flat—they had been very complimentary—he picked up his phone to speak to his PA.

He gave her the limited information he had, not doubting for a moment that she would be able to provide him with all the information he required; she was absolutely perfect, if you discounted the fact she was about to take maternity leave.

CHAPTER THREE

SOPHIE had not left work until 8:00 p.m. Taking advantage of the growing realisation that Sophie's work ethic was a little overdeveloped, people were dumping on her... *And what are you going to do about that?* asked the voice in her head.

It was a good question but one she had so far avoided; it wasn't as if her evening had contained any contemplative moments for reflection. She had arrived home to find a large hole in the street outside her flat, and after she'd pretended not to hear the comments about her bottom made by the men inside the hole, she discovered no water or electricity inside her flat.

The electricity had finally come on at eleven; the water still hadn't. She stopped waiting at twelve, cleaned her teeth with bottled water, finally crawled into her bed and with a sigh of relief turned out the light—not just because every bone in her body ached with exhaustion, but because the bedroom looked better with the light out.

'Basic, but I have everything I need,' she had told her mother on the phone, 'and I'm very near work.'

The work part was playing out a lot better than she had anticipated.

Conversations no longer stopped when she walked into room. Now that had not been nice, but even when she was viewed with extreme suspicion Sophie had kept her head down, concentrated on doing her best no matter how menial the task and smiled at everyone.

The hostility had faded once her co-workers had recognised she was not afraid of hard work—or, possibly, once they had recognised that there was someone who would willingly perform all the tasks nobody else wanted to do while smiling.

Sophie in her turn had discovered something too—she had a real talent for organisation; not quite the artistic spreading of wings her father had intended, but it was a start. She still felt homesick almost all the time but she didn't allow herself to think about going home.

She dreamt, though—she dreamt of her mum in the kitchen with flour in her nose, the smell of baking in the air... She was having that dream when the shrill sound of the phone cut through the cosy picture of domesticity.

Sophie surfaced and flicked on the lamp before reaching for the phone and snarling crankily, 'Yes...?' into the receiver.

'Sophie, thank God you're there!'

Sophie, who couldn't imagine where else she'd be at this time of night, which on reflection made her one of the most tragic twenty-three-year-olds on the planet, pushed her tangled hair from her eyes and frowned.

'*Amber...?* Why are you calling me at...' She glanced at the clock, saw the time and sat up straight, her eyes wide with alarm. 'What's wrong?'

'Everything,' came the tragic response. 'But we can do this.'

Sophie who was suspicious of the use of the word *we* asked, 'What's happened?'

'Just listen, don't talk. You have to be on the flight to Palermo at five-thirty.'

Pretty sure she was the victim of some elaborate hoax— either that or Amber had been drinking—Sophie leaned back, yawned and said, 'Of course I do.'

Palermo was the clue; she had made the flight arrangements

for Amber herself, and the office had been buzzing for days with the news that they had been contacted by Marco Speranza—*the* Marco Speranza, people kept saying to Sophie, as though she thought she might be likely to mistake him for another Sicilian billionaire.

Obviously, they had not been personally contacted, but the fact that the invitation to tender for a contract to refurbish his ancestral home had been issued by Marco's own office had been enough to send the entire office into party mode.

Sophie privately called it mass hysteria, and also a little premature. 'How many others are tendering?' Her tentative enquiry had been ignored.

'Something this prestigious could *make* us,' Amber had said as she'd gathered her team together to plan a strategy and draw up plans for a refurb that would knock the utterly gorgeous man's socks off.

Sophie, who was listening, would have loved to dispute the reverential *gorgeous* and the *utterly* but she had seen the photo someone had pinned on the notice board and there was no doubt at all that Marco Speranza was almost too good-looking to be real, unless he had been airbrushed to perfection.

The possibility made her feel unaccountably more cheerful.

Having worked her team into a state of hysterical enthusiasm Amber then smiled and promised, 'We are going to bury the opposition.'

Sophie's role in the team involved making tea but she had listened and frankly she had doubts, but aware that her place in the scheme of things did not involve giving an opinion she kept her mouth shut.

Sophie slid back under the covers as a sigh of relief echoed down the line. 'You know, Sophie, when I first saw you I thought…' Clearly thinking better of being that frank, Amber allowed herself a generous, 'You're an asset.'

'Thank you.' Now go away; I want to go to sleep.

'And I really admire your ability to multitask—maybe you could pack while we talk…?'

'Look, Amber, I'm going back to sleep now. I'll laugh at the joke tomorrow, and good luck with the Speranza contract.'

'No, Sophie, this isn't a joke. I can't go. This afternoon I—'

'You had a dentist's appointment. I know—it's in the diary.'

'No, I had some facial injections and a little liposuction on my thighs…at least, that was the idea, but it went wrong. I had a bad reaction to the anaesthetic and they won't let me go home—they took away my clothes!' she wailed.

Sophie's eyes widened at the confession. 'Relax, Amber, I'll contact Vincent.' Amber's right hand was up to speed and, if you overlooked his penchant for pink shirts, charming.

'Do you think I haven't already tried?' came the shrill response. 'He's gone to York! His partner's mum has had a heart attack and he's being supportive.'

Sophie, who had been introduced to Vincent's partner, said, 'Oh, how terrible. Colin must be—'

'Forget about Colin,' Amber yelled, 'and get packed.'

'But Sukie or Emma…' Sophie could hear the doubt in her own voice. The two women she had heard that first day discussing her both looked the part but neither had had an original thought in their lives.

'Emma is hopeless.'

You noticed! Sophie thought, surprised.

'And Sukie got dumped by her boyfriend and downed a bottle of Chardonnay to drown her sorrows. She is hanging over the toilet as we speak,' Amber observed bitterly.

Sophie grimaced and thought, Thanks for the image.

'And if you say "poor Sukie" I'll… My world is falling apart—my entire future depends on a girl who wears sensible shoes. No offence…' She sniffed between sobs.

The fact that Amber could weep made more of an impact on Sophie than either the insult or the apology.

'You're serious.' The realisation sent a rush of fear through her body. 'You want me to fly to Sicily and sell this to Marco Speranza's office?' This was what fairy tales were made of…or was that nightmares? Maybe she was still asleep and any minute she would wake up and laugh.

'Not his office—him.'

No, she was definitely awake; even her subconscious was not that inventive!

'I have a meeting with him personally which is why someone representing this firm *has* to be there. There is no option—we *need* this commission, Sophie. The credit crunch has been hard on everyone and I've had to write off a couple of big debts after the clients went under…'

About to cut her off and say there was just no way she could do this, something in the other woman's voice made Sophie pause… Oh, my God, she thought, as she realised what anyone who wasn't a spoilt, indulged rich kid who'd never had to think about money already would have.

This wasn't just about kudos. Amber was worried about her business's survival. Sophie was ashamed that she had been so wrapped up in her own concerns, so self-centred, that it hadn't even crossed her mind to wonder if maybe she wasn't the only one who had problems.

'You can't ask to reschedule a personal meeting with Marco Speranza.'

Sophie, thinking of her father, admitted, 'No, I can see that.' No man got to be that rich and powerful without taking a certain amount of deference for granted.

'If he thinks we've insulted him he could ruin my business. I've heard he can be utterly ruthless.' The sound of a sternly muffled sob echoed down the line.

Sophie heard the sob and folded. 'All right, I'll do it.'

Half an hour later she arrived at the office and collected the relevant papers and drawings from where Amber had said they'd be. She tucked them into her overnight bag, planning to read them on the flight.

'The idea will sell itself,' Amber had said.

God, I hope so, Sophie thought, because if they're relying on me we're stuffed!

'Isabella, many women come back to work the week after they've given birth or when they've had a Caesarean.'

His PA forgot her stately calm enough to laugh. 'Well, I'm not superwoman. I need six months and then I think we might discuss flexible hours.'

Marco put down the phone—the woman had him wound round her finger and she knew it, damn her!

Scowling to himself he left his car and walked into the lift. His temporary PA was scared of him, which might not have been a bad thing if this fear made her efficient, but it didn't. She gibbered and looked at him as though he was going to eat her and spoke so quietly he couldn't hear her.

And to make the situation worse he suspected his protégé was falling in love with her.

Love! Marco could not even think the word without a contemptuous sneer forming on his broad brow. Love did not mix well with the smooth running of his office. When he had spent the time and effort to groom Francesco he had taken an ability to keep his personal life separate from the demands of work as a given.

He did not seek to impose his views on his employees—what they did in their free time, including falling in love, did not concern him—but when love affairs crossed the line into the work place it became his concern.

When Marco walked into the office, Francesco broke off his conversation with the young woman whose fingers were flying across the keyboard.

Marco glanced their way but did not speak as he stalked towards the wall lined with files, impatience etched not just in every line of his startlingly good-looking face but in every tense muscle and sinew of his lean, athletic body.

He angled a sardonic brow. 'Did you want to see me, Francesco?' he asked, locating the file he was seeking and withdrawing it.

'No.'

Marco maintained a speaking silence, but though the younger man looked uncomfortable he did not look away. Marco gave a reluctant smile; his protégé was a fool but he was a fool who stood his ground, which was good. There was no place at a senior level for a man he could intimidate.

His smile faded when he turned his attention to the blushing young woman; incompetence always irritated him. 'I do not wish to be disturbed for the next two hours.'

'Oh, dear!'

Marco took his hand off the door handle of his office, stopped and swung back. *'Oh, dear?'* He angled a questioning brow and waited.

Francesco cleared his throat. 'Slight problem there. Your two-thirty has been here since, well...' He glanced at his wrist-watch which now read six-thirty. 'Well, two-thirty.'

Marco's brows drew into a disapproving straight line above the hawkish nose that bisected his chiselled features.

'I asked for you to reschedule.'

Again it was Francesco who spoke up. 'We tried, but we couldn't contact her in time. Miss Balfour had apparently lost her phone.'

Marco's expression accurately reflected his opinion of people who lost phones. 'My appointment was not with anyone called Balfour.'

'Well, that's who came.'

'And you put her in my office?' Marco's incredulous inter-rogative glare was directed towards his temporary secretary. 'You let a total stranger into my office?'

'That was my idea, Marco, when she wouldn't go away.'

'Wouldn't go away?' Marco echoed, his glance drifting towards the protective hand that Francesco had placed on the shoulder of his temporary secretary.

The expression in the girl's eyes seemed to confirm his worst suspicions. Great, he thought, just what I need—an office romance. Which means I either turn a blind eye or come the heavy and be about as popular as the plague.

Fortunately he did not need people to love him.

'When you say…*wouldn't go away*…'

The sardonic inflection in his boss's voice brought a flush to the younger man's face but he defended his decision and nodded.

'And frankly, I didn't have the heart to throw her out. The kid looked ready to cry when Analise—' he flashed a warm look at the seated woman and she blushed prettily '—suggested she could come back another day.'

'Kid?'

His secretary finally spoke up. 'My sister Toni is eighteen and she looks older than her.'

Marco, whose interest in her sister Toni was not immense, struggled to contain his growing impatience while Francesco added the weight of his opinion.

'She does look very young, Marco. She arrived direct from the airport and she'd lost her bags and she looked—'

'Pretty?' It was the other man's problem if he had a weakness for a pretty face, but when he allowed the Achilles heel to encroach into office hours it became a problem.

'No, not pretty,' Francesco said, struggling and failing to recall the features of the young English girl who had arrived looking scared stiff. 'She wasn't ugly or anything… Her eyes were blue,' he added, recalling the electric-blue eyes that had peeked out from under a long floppy fringe.

'Not pretty…I'm intrigued,' Marco drawled, sounding in reality both bored and irritated. 'Call her a cab.'

'I'll take her back to her hotel,' Francesco said to Marco's retreating back.

Marco turned and stared at his protégé with a perplexed expression. 'I suppose you gave her lunch too.'

'Sandwiches.'

'You're joking.'

In the office Marco saw that he had not been joking.

The crumbs on the plate testified to the meal.

CHAPTER FOUR

MARCO'S first view of his two-thirty was a hank of waving fairish hair hanging over the arm of a leather swivel chair that faced the window. Presumably the occupant was so busy looking at the view she had not heard him enter.

When he cleared his throat it did not cross his mind for an instant that his guest would not respond appropriately to the cue.

When she didn't, his aggravation levels climbed to a new high. His green eyes narrowed as he walked across the room; skirting the desk that stood between the chair and him he loosened his tie and said, 'This is not a convenient time. I must ask—'

His hand fell away from his throat and his dark brows tugged into a dark interrogative line. While he did not expect or enjoy people jumping to attention when he walked into a room, he was not accustomed to being ignored.

The frown still in place he walked around the desk and it became clear that his words had fallen on deaf ears, literally.

His two-thirty, her knees drawn up to her chest, her face cushioned on her hands, was fast asleep.

He studied her, and realised Francesco had not lied; she was very young and she was not pretty.

She was small, especially to a man who dated women who did not give him a pain in the neck to kiss, not that he felt any inclination to kiss his sleeping visitor awake.

Maybe there were men around who might have felt inclined to play the prince to her Sleeping Beauty but he doubted it.

Any curves, feminine or otherwise, were hidden in the capacious folds of the shapeless outfit that covered her, though her ankles were slim and her calves slender and shapely.

His view of her face was occluded by the messy mass of pale toffee-coloured hair that lay across her cheek. Her skin, slightly flushed with sleep, had the peachy smooth texture of extreme youth.

However, he did not make the mistake of equating youth with innocence; Allegra had not been much older than this girl when they had met, and her innocent sweetness had hidden a heart of pure malice.

Sophie opened her eyes and blinked, reluctant to relinquish her dream; she had been back home at the gatehouse, in her own room, and an ache of homesickness swelled in her chest.

She wasn't in Balfour, she was in Sicily, and awake, but the strong sense of disorientation lingered. Everything that could go wrong had; her luggage was probably in Outer Mongolia and that was the least of her problems.

The ache stayed where it was like a lead weight in her chest as she struggled to shrug off the last tenacious strands of sleep…maybe just a dream but it had felt so real.

She could still smell the vanilla of her mother's scones.

She inhaled and thought…not vanilla, something more subtly spicy and rather delicious. Pressing a hand to the back of her head as she tried to relieve the crick in her neck. She carefully unfolded her legs, causing the voluminous folds of her sprigged-cotton ankle-length skirt to bunch around her waist as she wriggled her toes.

About to reveal his presence Marco paused. His visitor might not be pretty and she might have a very odd taste in clothes, but she did have surprisingly good legs; if the creamy pallor of her flesh were any indication they had never seen the light of day.

He felt his curiosity stir—did that creamy pallor extend all over?

God, how long had she been asleep?

If Marco Speranza had walked in and found her snoring…that really would have made a great impression, she thought, cringing at the mental image. She stretched again, flexing the kinks out of her spine, then wincing as her elbow caught a jarring blow on the coffee pot on the table beside her.

'Oh, no!' she exclaimed, as the contents of the half-full pot fell with a crash to the floor where it shattered.

'Of *course*, it shattered—this is the day from hell!' Gritting her teeth Sophie fell on her knees beside the broken glass and spilled liquid that was becoming a spreading stain on the thick white carpet.

Sitting back on her heels she closed her eyes.

Despite a lot of wishing when she opened them again she was still there. Why, she wondered, patting the coffee stain ineffectually with a tissue from her pocket, do these things happen to me?

Marco, who had watched her waking moments up to this point in silence, decided it was necessary to intercede—before she sliced off a finger.

Stepping forward he took firm hold of the hand that held the shard of splintered glass.

'What?' Sophie turned her head and watched with saucer-wide eyes as the glass was removed from her fingers. Shock made her compliant as she was then pulled unceremoniously to her feet.

Sophie's wide gaze stayed on the long brown extremely strong fingers circling her wrist and continued upwards, moving over a section of golden-skinned forearm, dark against the pale cuff complete with discreet but obviously expensive cufflinks.

She had to tilt her head back to see the man who wore them and then as she met his eyes she immediately wished she hadn't made the effort. His eyes were green, deep dark green flecked with tiny specks of gold, and they regarded her with an air of critical disdain.

The sort of critical disdain reserved for the use of someone who was perfect—and physically, he was—when looking at someone who wasn't.

She had already known that Marco Speranza was good-looking, but neither the grainy tabloid shots of him on the notice board or the more glossy images in celebrity magazines had been able to convey just how good-looking he actually was.

They had not conveyed the restless vitality, the overpowering aura of raw masculinity he exuded. She had never encountered a man who was so blatantly sexual; just looking at him put very uncharacteristic thoughts into her head. She had never in her life looked at a stranger's mouth and wondered what it would feel like to be kissed by him.

Sophie had spent a lot of time around beautiful people, but the man currently regarding her with an air of irritated disdain was something *very* special.

He was the most beautiful creature she had ever seen.

'You're late,' she blurted, the second thing that popped into her head; it could have been worse, as the first had been, *Are you a good kisser?*

One dark brow sketched upwards as he released her hand. 'I am so sorry to have kept you waiting.'

Sophie nursed her hand against her chest. The impression his fingers left on her skin was so real that she expected to see the imprint glowing like a brand.

The skin on her narrow wrist was pale and unblemished.

Some of Amber's advice came back to her. 'You're a woman, Sophie…' Midway through, her boss had stopped short, maybe reconsidering the statement before adding, 'Men always respond well to subtle flattery. You have to stroke their egos.'

The woman had clearly never met Marco Speranza! His ego was probably so massive that she doubted she could reach it.

'I'm sorry. I fell asleep.'

'I noticed.' His sardonic tone made her flush in embarrassment and she bit her lip and wondered, *Was my mouth open? Have I been drooling?*

She watched uncertainly as Marco Speranza lowered himself into the leather chair behind his big desk and opened his laptop, and decided upon reflection it was better she didn't know.

'I'm sorry you had a wasted journey,' he said, not looking at her.

She regarded his dark head with dismay. 'That's it…you're not interested in my ideas?'

He leaned back in his chair and, pushing it back from the desk, looked at her through hooded eyes. 'I only deal with serious professionals.'

'I'm…*we're* serious professionals,' she protested.

He gave a thin-lipped smile and shook his head. 'I don't think so.'

'But!'

'Your firm sent *you*.' His green eyes swept upwards from her feet to her face. He gave a fluid shrug and turned his attention back to the computer screen. Then as if he changed his mind he lifted his head and added, 'They sent a child. I'd say that that gives me a very good idea at how seriously your firm wants this job.'

'I'm twenty-three and I assure you I'm qualified, Mr Speranza.'

He gave another languid shrug and drawled, 'I will take your word on both counts.' Though the twenty-three part still seemed doubtful to him.

His attention refocused on the screen of the open laptop on his desk; he was not looking at her.

For Marco Speranza she no longer existed.

Keeping her head up Sophie took a step towards the door. She could retain what shred of dignity she had left and be graceful in defeat.

What was the point in fighting?

Marco Speranza had made up his mind the moment he laid eyes on her. She had taken two steps when she realised she was falling back into a pattern of behaviour—graceful defeat translated as failure.

Her father had faith in her; her sisters would not have wimped out this way but she wasn't even trying. They'd all be kind when she crawled back with her tail between her legs but she knew that privately they'd be disappointed.

What did she have to lose?

The frustration welled up inside her and expanded, a solid presence in her chest, until she felt as though she couldn't breathe.

Jaw set she turned and walked back to the desk. 'You haven't given me a chance!' she accused loudly.

Marco Speranza's eyes lifted from the laptop.

The astonishment in his face might on another occasion have made her laugh, but Sophie, who was hearing the disappointment in her father's voice when he realised his faith in her had been misplaced, planted her hands on her hips.

'Well, did you?' she demanded belligerently. 'You wrote me off the moment you walked in here.'

The hands-on-the-hip stance was not good when you did not want to draw attention to their unfortunate width, but Sophie was beyond caring if he thought she was chunky. Chances were he had not even noticed she was female, let alone that she had horribly generous curves.

He didn't bother denying it. 'I do that when people are so committed they fall asleep. And can you really expect to be taken seriously, appearing in someone's office dressed as you are?' He stopped twirling the pen in his long fingers and laid it on the table. 'You know, I think you'll go farther if you invest in a comb…' he mused.

Her cobalt-blue eyes—the intense colour reminded him of the sea along the Ionian coast—slid from his and as he watched she bit into her trembling lower lip.

Marco suddenly felt less than thrilled with his clever comeback; the moment he had allowed things to become personal he had lost the moral and every other sort of high ground. This English girl was enough to try the patience of a saint, but nothing excused behaviour that had drifted worryingly close to bullying.

'Look, if you have notes, sketches, leave them. I will look at them and get back to your boss.'

Anticipating a certain amount of tearful gratitude for his generous compromise he was taken aback when the eyes that lifted slowly to his were not misty with gratitude but sparking with anger.

'How dare you patronise me!'

Sophie's first reaction to his scathing put-down had been to laugh, then with a sudden flash of insight she realised that this was yet another coping mechanism.

People had been making her a joke all her life, and she had been letting them. She had been telling herself she didn't care.

Sophie suddenly realised she did care—she cared a lot.

'Patronise!' This woman gave *unreasonable* a whole new meaning.

'All you've done is sneer and look down your nose at me. People like you make me sick—people who think they are entitled to what they want, when they want it, just because of what their name is. Well, I hate that world and I don't want to live in it.'

'Where do you want to live?'

Sophie's blue eyes narrowed warily. 'We are not talking about me.'

'My mistake,' Marco drawled, thinking that even if she had a presentation that was mind-blowing he would be insane to take someone on his payroll who had such obvious issues. 'Do you ever pause for breath when you speak?'

'I only babble when I get nervous.'

'And I make you nervous?'

She glared and thought, You'd like that, wouldn't you? 'You make me…' She stopped, conscious of something that bore a worrying similarity to exhilaration circulating in her veins.

She was not enjoying this! He was a horrible man and she hated arguing. He was just so convinced he was right, when in reality he was so wide of the mark that he was not even on the right page. The man was infuriating.

'You only value things that are beautiful.'

He blinked at the accusation.

'You!' she declared, waving a condemnatory finger at him. 'Judge by appearances…!' The last time she'd said this much was when she had drank too much—if two glasses of champagne deserved that title—after her nephew Oliver's christening.

She had fallen into the fountain; people were still teasing her about it.

The transformation from mouse-like timidity to bristling bosom-heaving antagonism interested Marco as much as the charge.

'What else am I meant to judge you on?' he asked, watching the finger that was being waved in his direction and thinking appearances in this instance were definitely deceptive.

This reasonable question made Sophie pause. 'You said my outfit meant you couldn't take me seriously.'

'That was rude—I was out of order, but I've had a bad day.'

'*You've* had a bad day!' she squeaked, throwing up her hands. '*You,*' she told him with husky quivering emphasis, 'know *nothing* about bad days, and for your information it's nothing to do with my clothes. I have sisters, as I'm sure you know, who could make a bin sack look fashionable and sexy.'

'So you decided not to compete.'

Her mouth was already open to refute the ludicrous claim, but a look of doubt spread slowly across Sophie's face. She closed her mouth with a snap. It wasn't true...*was it*? The man was a total stranger; how could he have a clue as to what made her tick?

'It's not about competition, it's about recognising I'm not...' An image of her sisters flashed before her eyes, each beautiful and talented in their own unique and very photogenic way, and she thought again, Is he right?

With a tiny shake of her head she dismissed the idea and stuck out her chin.

'I'm not like them.' If she was, he wouldn't be ignoring her...only he wasn't; there was an interest of the clinical variety in the green eyes that rested on her flushed face.

'Why are you sure I know you have sisters?'

'Because I'm a Balfour.' His blank expression was not one that Sophie had ever encountered previously after revealing her identity. Thrown by the response, her next words held a note of disbelief. 'My father is Oscar Balfour.'

Sophie gave a self-deprecating shrug that turned out to be unneeded. Marco Speranza's brows lifted in recognition of the name, though he still did not look impressed.

'I have never met the man, though obviously I know his reputation. I'm sure I would be more au fait with your sisters if I read the sort of scandal sheets that chart their exploits.'

'Well, *you* appear in them often enough!' Sophie retorted, stung by his superior attitude. Before their break up, he and his gorgeous wife must have been one of the most photographed couples on the planet. 'And my sisters do not ask to be photographed.' Though admittedly they did not go out of their way to avoid it either.

'Why are we discussing your sisters?'

Sophie looked at him, nonplussed by the question. Over the years she had become philosophical about men seeking her out for this specific reason and here was one who sounded bored by the subject. If he had been displaying any more interest in her it would have been her dream scenario.

But he wasn't.

In fact, playing the Balfour card had not given her any advantage with this man.

'I'm sure your sisters are fascinating, but right now—' he glanced significantly at the watch on his wrist and turned back to his laptop '—I have several items that require my attention.'

Sophie stemmed the flow of anger with a firm shake of her head, the action causing a glossy hank of hair she had just secured behind her ear to fall into her eyes, and with an impatient grimace she pushed it back with her forearm from her flushed cheek before anchoring it once again behind her ear. She gritted her teeth. 'God, I think I might just cut it all off.'

'Your hair?'

'You're not interested in my hair and you're not interested on what's inside—yes, I get that,' she told him, thinking that the last thing she wanted was Marco Speranza with his disturbing eyes being privy to her insecurities.

'You really don't need to labour the point, and as for what you should judge me on, how about—and I know this might be a novel idea—ability?' The sarcasm faded from her voice as she added, 'Unless you get some kind of kick out of making people feel inadequate and stupid!'

The emotional throb in her voice dragged Marco's attention from her thick hair that on closer scrutiny proved not to be one colour but interwoven strands of several colours that ran the spectrum from soft butter gold to pale coffee.

His fingers flexed on the polished surface of his desk as he suddenly imagined spearing his fingers into the lush mass. 'You wouldn't suit short hair.'

Startled by the husky observation she lifted a hand to her head.

His green eyes returned to the wild waves. 'A trim possibly,' he conceded.

Sophie shook her head. Why were they talking about her hair? 'Are you trying to be funny?'

She watched a flicker of some emotion, impossible to decipher, ripple across the reflective surface of his remarkable green eyes before he shrugged.

'I'm making a constructive comment. Is the colour real?'

Baffled by his question and suspecting some sort of hidden insult, Sophie said defiantly, 'Yes. This is all me.' She flashed him a cold look that tipped into confusion as their glances connected. 'Take me or leave me,' she finished breathlessly.

CHAPTER FIVE

She saw the startled look spread across his face and realised she had just given him the opening for a massive put-down.

Her heart raced with a confusing cocktail of emotions—trepidation, proving she had not totally lost it; exhilaration, proving it was a close-run thing. *If he laughs I will die of sheer mortification,* she thought, but he didn't laugh.

He didn't actually do anything.

'Not literally,' she hastened to assure him. 'I wasn't…' She cleared her throat and added awkwardly, 'Propositioning you.'

Observing the faint twitching of his sensually sculpted mobile lips, Sophie was discovering that for some inexplicable reason his mouth exerted an almost magnetic pull. He's thinking what a great story to produce at a dull moment during a dinner party, she thought. This dumpy, dowdy Balfour chick asked me to *take* her. Well, maybe not *chick*; she couldn't really see Marco Speranza saying *chick* in that deep sexy Italian accent of his.

Of course, if she'd been sleek and glossy and had long legs and wore a short skirt he wouldn't have been laughing. If she had been any other Balfour girl he wouldn't have been laughing.

Not that he actually was laughing, she realised, studying his face and wondering if wanting to know what it felt like to be lusted after just once in her life made her very shallow or just human.

When he finally responded there was no hint of the amusement she had anticipated in his dry comeback. 'I think I'm disappointed.'

She knew he was being sarcastic but it didn't show on his face. His expression was about as easy to read as a granite wall but much, *much* better to look at.

Sophie realised she was staring at his sensual mouth again and, after a struggle, managed to redirect her gaze to the open neck of his shirt where the skin of his throat was smooth and bronzed a tasty…no, *toasty* gold.

The mental correction brought a wary expression to her face as she tried to smile through the shocking stab of lustful longing that took her totally unawares.

She was obviously in desperate need of a sugar hit.

Deciding it was certainly necessary to bring this meeting to a speedy close, Sophie inhaled deeply and pinned a sympathetic expression on her face. 'Look, I know you're probably upset that Amber didn't attend this meeting in person.'

'Because the male of the species has a fragile ego?'

Biting back a snippy retort, Sophie smiled. 'But you really should see what we have to offer. I'm sure you'll be impressed.'

She watched him flick through the corners of the file she had brought and scroll his way through the pages; he did not look impressed.

'Boring, bland and predictable.'

Sophie was in a dilemma; she actually agreed with his scathing assessment, but she wasn't here to preserve her artistic integrity. She was here to save Amber's business and everyone else's job, and if in the process she proved to her dad that she was more than just a dreamer it would be a massive bonus.

'First impressions can be wrong.'

Marco, who had been thinking much the same thing himself, inclined his head. 'You think so.'

'I know so,' she retorted firmly. 'And of course that is just a rough draft. Amber always involves the client, any client—and you're not just any client; you're a very important man.' Though clearly not as important as you think you are, she thought, injecting several more volts of false sincerity into her fixed smile.

The rather startling realisation that he was being patronised slowed Marco's response.

'She was devastated that she couldn't be here. I wasn't the first choice to make this pitch, or even,' she admitted, 'the second.'

Sophie had doubts about honesty being the best policy but at this point it seemed she had little to lose by being frank, and the novelty value might even get his attention.

It did, but as those laser-sharp green eyes stilled on her face, she wasn't so sure this was necessarily a good thing.

'So Miss…Amber…intended to come personally. But despite my…*extreme* importance she is not here.' And her substitute had a very unique sales pitch. The disingenuous act could not possibly be genuine but he had to admit it did have the charm of being not boring.

'She's not…well, actually her liposuction went wonky.' Sophie was unable to repress a shudder at the mental image. Then realising her frankness might just have tipped over into indiscretion, she tacked on quickly, 'It was a very minor procedure—people have it done in their lunch hour these days.'

'I take it you do not speak from personal experience.'

His eyes slid to her legs, now totally obscured by the voluminous skirt and a top that reached her knees, but what he had already seen made it obvious that this was not a procedure that she needed.

But then women frequently endured painful procedures to measure up to some weird ideal of perfection. There was no such thing as perfection, though that glimpse of soft creamy skin on her thighs was actually pretty close.

He was looking at her thighs when he spoke, which just went to prove that the man didn't have a tactful bone in his quite magnificent body. Outraged all over again at his rudeness and without stopping to think, Sophie snapped, 'I'm happy with my body the way it is! But of course if I wasn't all right with it, and I didn't already know I was fat, that comment might have hurt!'

Had she just rapped his knuckles? Marco couldn't decide; he had very little room for comparison as it had been many years since even his closest friends had admonished him.

Embarrassed by her outburst—what on earth had got into her?—Sophie screwed up her courage and plunged on. If this was a lost cause, at least she wouldn't go quietly.

She heard herself say, 'I'm actually very good.'

'At what?'

At least he hadn't laughed but Sophie, who had already been cringing at her boastful claim, felt panic....

'I may not have a lot of experience...' You're telling him this...why, exactly?

'No experience...there's a shocker.'

'But that's an advantage.'

'It is?' Marco found he no longer had to feign fascination.

'Well, I'm open to new ideas. I've not got a closed mind.'

'Give me an example of your open mind.'

Sophie smiled; if he thought that was going to throw her he could think again. Finally, she could talk about something she knew about.

'Well, for starters, look at this room.' Sophie's nose wrinkled as her sweeping gesture took in the large oblong space.

His brows lifted; he was almost enjoying himself now. This was unlike any conversation he had had with a woman before. 'It is not to your liking?'

'It's all right,' she conceded with a sniff. 'But do you want *all right* for your ancestral home?' she asked, levelling a challenging look at his face, which gave her precisely zero clues to what he felt about her tactics.

'I don't do *all right*!' Recognising she hadn't even felt embarrassed saying this, Sophie wondered if it was something to do with lack of sleep or possibly the fact that every time she looked at Marco Speranza she felt the prickles of antagonism trickle down her spine.

It was irrational to so dislike someone she barely knew.

Marco leaned deeper into his chair and, stretching his long legs out in front of him, crossed one ankle over the other before fixing his hooded gaze on her flushed face.

'What do you do, Miss Balfour?'

'I do *exceptional*.' This is insane—Sophie, what are you doing?

'Exceptional? I'm impressed.' One corner of his mouth lifted as he smiled and rested his chin on the platform provided by his steepled fingers. 'Well, don't stop now…'

Now genuinely intrigued, Marco pushed his chair from the table and rose to his feet in one fluid motion. 'I must admit, I thought I already had exceptional.'

I really wish he'd stayed sitting, Sophie thought as she watched him move across the room, looking like the human version of a jungle cat—elegant, dangerous and casually cruel—until he stood framed by the window with the breathtaking panoramic view of the Old City below.

Not that Sophie was looking at the view. Marco had what could be called presence. Unable to dispel the lithe-jungle-cat analogy, she saw herself in the role of the pathetic defenceless animal he swatted just for the hell of it, and her courage wavered.

You're not defenceless, you're a *Balfour*! Show a bit of backbone for once!

Balfours rose to the challenge and it was encouraging that he hadn't thrown her out yet…possibly just because he enjoyed seeing her squirm, but there was a possibility, outside admittedly, that this wasn't lost yet.

'So how would you make this space exceptional?'

'Well, to begin with,' she said, banging her hand on the wall behind her, 'this would go, as well as those windows.' As she continued to outline the changes she would make, her nervousness receded. She knew what she was talking about and her genuine enthusiasm made it surprisingly easy to articulate her creative ideas to someone who was listening with what seemed like genuine interest. Of course, he might just be waiting to pull her legs from under her with one cutting remark, but with the adrenaline buzz humming through her veins Sophie thought it was a risk worth taking.

What do I have to lose? she asked herself. She pushed past the recognition that at one level she was actually enjoying herself—it was just too bizarre.

Marco watched her as she moved around the room, illustrating her suggestions with gestures, speaking with increasing confidence as the ideas flowed. The change in her demeanour was nothing less than spectacular.

Her entire manner, voice and body language had altered. Gone was the awkward self-conscious hunched-shoulder attitude; her voice was animated, her blue eyes sparkled with enthusiasm—an enthusiasm that was so obviously genuine that Marco found himself smiling.

Slick patter and dodgy figures left him cold but he was drawn to the thing that was, in his experience, rare—a mix of genuine enthusiasm, talent and passion.

Sophie Balfour was a revelation.

'Well, that's what I think anyway,' Sophie said, finally drawing breath as she removed her hand from the wall she had just verbally demolished. 'The glass would make the most of the marvellous light and the sleek modern lines of the furniture…' Her voice faded as without warning her knees began to shake.

Actually, she was shaking all over.

CHAPTER SIX

IT WAS very confusing; one moment he was propped up against the window with languid ease, and the next Marco Speranza was at her side, his hand on her shoulder as he forced her into a Phillipe Starck chair.

Actually, there was very little force involved. Her knees folded; it had been a *very* long day.

'Nice chair.' Sophie was not sure if she spoke out loud or not. 'But not in here.' A great piece but it just didn't mesh with the rest of the decor.

'Always the critic. Water.' She had lost all colour and her intense pallor brought the vivid blue of her eyes into sharp contrast.

His lean dark features blurred before her eyes as she shook her head; even blurred he looked pretty incredible. 'I'm not thirsty.'

'If you drink this I will burn the damn chair.' Marco took her fingers and folded them around the glass before guiding it to her lips and saying harshly, 'Drink!'

Left with little choice she obeyed him.

'Better?' he asked, touching his thumb to a small trickle of water at the corner of her mouth.

The soft touch sent a secret shiver down her spine. 'I'm fine,' she said, hoping that the breathiness in her voice was down to her wobbly moment and not the light touch.

Much to Sophie's relief his hand fell away from her face,

but his disturbing hard emerald gaze lingered another few uncomfortable moments on her mouth.

'Well, you don't look it.'

Her chin went up. 'I'm fine,' she insisted, utterly mortified
by this display of weakness. 'Totally fine. I just… Don't burn
the chair—it's very nice…'

'But it offends your aesthetic sensitivities in this setting.'

'I'm not sensitive.' As to contradict this statement her nerve
endings acted in an inappropriate and over-the-top—actually
painful—way to the faint brush of his fingertips against the inside
of her wrist as he relinquished his supportive grip on the glass.

'I don't make a habit of *almost* fainting. It's just…I can't
skip meals.'

She seemed perfectly serious and Marco, who was accustomed to women who only ate carbs on days without a *D* in
them, glanced towards the crumbs on the empty plate.

Sophie intercepted the direction of his gaze and said defen-
sively, 'That was not a proper meal—it was sandwiches.'

The twitch of his lips suggested she was about to lose the
credibility she had struggled so hard to establish so Sophie
plunged on without pause, veering sharply away from the
subject of her appetite that was as unfashionable as her figure.

'We can do the job, and we can do it well. Check out our
track record.'

He still looked distracted, probably shocked by the idea of
a woman actually eating… The article she had read on the plane
had included a large and growing back catalogue of disposable
girlfriends, none of whom looked like they had ever eaten a full
meal in their lives. Clearly, they considered starvation not too
high a price to pay for being seen on the arm of someone as
famous and rich as Marco Speranza, she thought cynically.

Her cynicism wobbled slightly as her glance moved over the
strong angular contours of his face, coming to rest on the firm
sensual curve of his mouth.

He had money and fame but he also had animal magnetism oozing out of his perfect pores—and he had that mouth.

Maybe they weren't so stupid.

You're staring at his mouth, Sophie.

Maybe he's just very good in bed?

Focus, Sophie, she told herself as she dodged his gaze and brushed an invisible speck from her creased and crumpled jacket.

He wasn't a mind reader; it just *seemed* as if those eerie green eyes of his—no man should have eyelashes that long—could see into her head. Still, if he even suspected that she was wondering, even in a dispassionate sort of way, about his sexual performance…!

Sophie cleared her throat and said in her best professional voice 'You won't find a firm that is better or more innovative.'

'Promises are cheap,' Marco said, thinking that her sultry, husky little voice just didn't match the rest of her, though her lips, cherry red in her pale face, did have possibilities. She had the sort of complexion that a Victorian lady would have given her best ostrich feather to possess.

'We are not.' Pleased with her swift retort she gave a regal smile and added, 'You pay for quality.' There was nothing Sophie liked better than a bargain.

'And if you don't give us a chance it will be your loss!' she warned, thinking, *Mine too*, as she crossed her fingers.

Marco, who had been studying his interlinked fingers, suddenly looked down and held her eyes.

The moment probably only lasted a moment but for Sophie, with a bucketful of heart-racing adrenaline still swirling in her veins and her nerve stretched to breaking point, it felt like a lifetime.

'Look, I meant it—I don't make a habit of having dizzy spells, and contrary to appearances I happen to be a very organised person.' Organisation was the one thing she could do, and to see the scepticism on his face was tough to swallow.

But she wasn't here to court Marco Speranza's good opinion. This wasn't personal—it didn't matter what Marco Speranza thought of her; it mattered that he signed on the dotted line and she chalked up lots of brownie points.

It mattered that she lived up to the confidence her father had in her.

'But this isn't about me—I'm just the messenger.' Wasn't it the messenger that got shot? 'You wouldn't have to see me at all.'

He didn't look as relieved as she had anticipated. Maybe he didn't believe her? 'I'm strictly a back-room person.' If she pulled this off, that might change. She felt a surprising spurt of excitement at a possibility that would have once given her nightmares.

'You make it sound as though they keep you in a cupboard. Do they let you out on special occasions?

Sophie smiled, assuming he didn't expect her to reply to this frivolous comment.

Don't look too desperate, Sophie…desperate is not a good sales tool, she told herself as she met his eyes projecting, she sincerely hoped, professional competence.

Siren sex appeal might have been more effective, she thought with a silent sigh, but a girl had to use what she had.

Her smile stayed painted in place as she watched under the sweep of her lashes as he walked across to his desk.

He closed the lid of the laptop with a decisive click and lifted his head. 'All right,' he said slowly.

Sophie's jaw dropped.

She looked, he reflected, as surprised as he felt to hear his response.

It wasn't one thing that had changed his mind but a combination; the plans were rubbish but she had ideas and enthusiasm.

She has what you have lost, Marco—she has passion!

And nice legs—*excellent* legs.

Sophie stared at him warily. 'We've got the job?'

Marco angled a brow. 'Do you want it?'

A wide smile spread across her pale features, transforming her face into a vision of sparkling animation as she jumped to her feet.

'Yes, of course, that's…that's just… You won't be sorry, Mr Speranza,' she said eagerly as she grabbed his hand between the two of her own and pumped it up and down. Then, aware he was looking at her very strangely, she dropped it and gave a self-conscious shrug. 'Sorry, I'm just so happy.'

'Before you spontaneously combust I must tell you there is one condition.'

Sophie's smile stayed glued in place but her eyes were wary. *I should have known there was going to be a catch*, she thought, deciding whatever he asks for no matter how preposterous nod and say yes. He's the client—just remember, Sophie, the customer is always right.

'I reserve the right to terminate the arrangement if I am not happy.'

'Of course.' Sophie pulled out her notebook and turned to a fresh page.

'And you will personally oversee the project.'

Sophie assumed she had misheard. 'Sorry, I didn't quite…'

'I wish for you to personally oversee the project.'

Sophie looked up. She made herself smile at his joke and tilted her head back to look up into his lean face, her eyes drawn to the small scar beside his mouth—the only flaw in his otherwise perfect face—and she wondered how he got it.

'Seriously, Mr Speranza, I'm sure we can accommodate all your needs.'

The earnest assurance brought Marco's gaze to her face. 'That is good to know,' he drawled.

Sophie recognised the amused glint in his eyes and translated his drawled retort as *thanks but no thanks*.

Sarcastic rat!

She schooled her features into a neutral mask; the mortified flush that rose up her neck until her entire face burned she had no control over.

'I admire confidence in a woman, Miss Balfour.'

Not half as much as he admired long legs and making love naked on a beach, if his ex-wife's no-holds-barred account of their passionate marriage in a recent interview in a celebrity publication was anything to go by.

'However, I don't think you'd know where to begin,' he said, although…what did they say about still waters running deep? It was possible that prim exterior hid a fiery and passionate nature.

Possible but not likely, though that mouth…?

Even though Sophie knew he wasn't serious, she couldn't help imagining what it would feel like to be presented with such an opportunity. It could make a person's career or, of course, break it if you blew it or got sacked, but she didn't have to worry about that. She had done what was asked of her—she had got him. She still couldn't figure out what had swung the decision in her favour, but the worry and the kudos were all her boss's—and Amber was welcome to it, and to the pleasure of being forced to smile at this man with an ego that matched the size of his bank balance.

'Seriously, Mr Speranza…'

'Seriously, Miss Balfour.'

'No…no…I mean, that's not possible. I don't do that sort of thing. I'm very junior and I only got the job because Amber had a thing with my dad.'

During the pause that followed her disclosure—way too much information, Sophie—she tried without success to read his expression.

'My,' he drawled. 'You really know how to sell yourself, don't you?'

This time she could read his expression and, while she generally had no problem laughing at herself, when the person she'd be joining in with was this man, all she could manage was a clenched smile.

'I'm working on it,' she gritted through her teeth.

'I heard the British upper classes don't move their mouths when they speak…' And in her case it was a pretty mouth. 'But until now I didn't believe it.' He leaned back in his hair with languid ease. 'One of the reasons I didn't show you the door—'

Sophie waited for the punchline and when it didn't come said, 'Because I'm underqualified but well connected?'

'—is because you don't say what I want to hear.'

'I was trying to,' she retorted with feeling.

Marco threw back his head and laughed.

Hearing the deep husky sound the couple in the adjoining office, who had been debating whether to go in and see what was happening, exchanged startled looks.

Sophie, who had no idea that Marco Speranza laughing in the work place was not a usual event, was startled for other reasons—Marco Speranza had a sense of humour!

That and a low, husky, uninhibited laugh that made the downy hair on her skin stand on end. Laughter softened the lines of his austerely beautiful face and made him look younger and almost approachable.

'One? What were the others?'

There was a pause as he appeared to consider the question and her face.

Sophie found his unblinking scrutiny deeply unsettling.

'You don't carry any baggage… You're fresh…'

The situation would change; experience would put cynicism in her eyes and etch lines onto her smooth skin, but right now her eyes were clear…and her skin… Feeling suddenly, incredibly old and jaundiced, he felt an unexpected stab of something that was close to envy.

When had he last experienced the sort of enthusiasm that shone in her eyes?

'People in your profession frequently fall into the trap of thinking in terms of what is fashionable. I am not interested in the latest colour charts—I feel passionate about my home,' he declared, feeling hypocritical.

The fact was he was not capable about feeling passionate about anything. During his marriage he had become adept at hiding his feelings from his spiteful wife, who got a sick kick out of inflicting pain. At some point he hadn't needed to hide them any more as there hadn't been anything to hide.

Had those feelings died or were they in cold storage? The fact that he was capable of objectively considering each possibility made Marco suspect the former was true.

'I want someone to work on it who is capable of…' He paused and thought, *Capable of reminding me how I once felt.* His eyes slid from her face and he said abruptly, 'I am a Sicilian.'

As if that said it all. 'I'm not.'

Marco's glance drifted to her mouth and he felt things shift inside him. 'You spoke very eloquently, with passion.'

'That wasn't passion, that was desperation.'

A flicker of irritation crossed his lean face but some of the tension left his shoulders. 'This constant self-deprecation can get wearing.' However, looking at her mouth did not.

Sophie opened her mouth to retort and closed it again, not because she'd just remembered he was the client and the client was always right, but because *he* was right.

It had started as a protective mechanism—get in there before someone else did. Endless casual comments, not normally intended to wound, about her figure, her hair, her lack of small talk… The list was endless and they did hurt, so it was now almost a reflex to pull herself down before anyone else got the chance.

It was ironic that the person to open her eyes was a total stranger—and *this* total stranger.

Aiming somewhere midway between pushy and motivated she gave him a direct look. 'You're serious.'

He gave the appearance of considering the question. 'Those are my conditions.'

'Even if I could, Amber would never agree. You've probably already noticed I'm not a front-of-shop person.' Her sweeping gesture took in her creased outfit. 'I source materials and deal with orders and make sure that… In short, I make lists,' Sophie explained, frowning at the somewhat lame job description she had produced. 'I'm very good at lists.'

'You mean you do the work and let others take the credit.' His expression did not suggest he found such a self-sacrificing mentality admirable, and his scorn stung.

Easy for him, she thought. He walked into a room and everything about him screamed dominant male; he didn't have a clue what it felt like to be invisible among her dazzling siblings. As much as she loved them, they were overwhelming.

She felt her resentment rise as she studied his chiselled patrician features. Marco Speranza didn't have the faintest idea what it felt like to blend into the background, and anyway it wasn't even true—she wasn't a doormat!

Her indignation was mixed with unease—was that really the impression she gave?

'Just because I don't need to be the centre of attention doesn't make me a total doormat.'

Encountering the hostile glitter in her blue eyes Marco smiled.

'What's so funny?' she asked between clenched teeth as she endured his searching stare.

'Not a doormat…afraid.' He taunted. He watched her chin go up and smiled. Getting the best out of people in his experience was about providing the correct motivation and knowing which buttons to push.

Sophie avoided arguments and confrontations—she disliked raised voices—but she suddenly realised that there were occasions when a person had to stand up and be counted…or explode!

Her hands balled into fists at her sides.

Dear God, the man was a total stranger and he was acting as if he knew her. First her father, and then this man, telling her what was wrong with her—well, she was sick of it! She was so mad she could hardly see straight as she fixed him with a glittering blue scowl.

'I'm not afraid!' she yelled. 'Not all of us need to have people telling us how marvellous we are every two seconds. I don't need my ego stroked to make me feel good about myself, unlike some people.'

A look of utter amazement crossed Marco's face; he had obviously pressed more buttons than he had intended. He studied her with renewed interest—she was definitely not lacking the passion he required.

He arched a brow. 'Some people?'

Sophie, her chest heaving, allowed her lashes to fall in a concealing curtain over her eyes; the silence that settled between them was as loud as a slamming door.

The door was probably slamming on her career.

She couldn't believe she had actually said those things. It was, she reflected, as if another person had taken over her body. And even more bewildering than this emergence of another persona was the adrenaline rush—her body still hummed with it.

Was it the man or the circumstances that were making her act this way?

Sophie tried to smooth things over. Not that she really expected to succeed; a man like Marco Speranza would never let a mere employee speak to him that way. 'I don't want to make this personal.' Pity, Sophie, you didn't think that way a minute ago.

'Do *you* want the job?'

'Do I want the job?' Sophie echoed. 'After what I just said?' She was unable to hide her amazement. 'But I thought...'

'Thought or hoped?' he asked with a sardonic smile. He

thought that he had seen every interview technique but hers was, he had to admit, unique.

He did not surround himself with yes-men but Marco couldn't recall the last time that someone had challenged him in the work place. A man who wasn't challenged was in danger of becoming complacent and losing his edge.

'I made a personal comment, and you responded. So long as you do not forget who's the boss, I think we will deal well together…'

Laughter bubbled up in her throat. 'I don't think it's likely you'll let me.'

'Do you want the job?' His lashes lifted from the angle of his sharply defined razor-edged cheekbones as he scanned her face. 'If not, there is little point us continuing this discussion.'

'Yes!' Sophie heard herself shout, then more moderately and ignoring the voice in her head asking, Are you totally insane? she added, 'I would like the job, Mr Speranza.' This so *wasn't* going to happen. Amber would voluntarily break a fingernail before she'd let Sophie take control of such a prestigious project.

As if reading her thoughts—that ability was getting distinctly unsettling—Marco moved around his desk, balanced on a corner and stretched his long legs out in front of him. 'Leave your boss to me.' He rose to his feet, tipped his dark head. 'Come…'

This autocratic decree made Sophie stare—was this man for real?

He didn't snap his fingers but the expectation was much the same. He was clearly accustomed to unquestioning obedience and the force of his personality was such that she suspected he generally got it.

The man had an egotism that made her father look mild mannered and hesitant by comparison.

'Where?' she said, not moving.

He looked mildly irritated by the question. 'I have a home to go to if you don't, Miss Balfour.'

He watched her get to her feet and wondered what he had said to fill her expressive eyes with bleak pain? He placed a hand between her shoulder blades and repeated his command. 'Come.' But this time his manner was gentler.

Sophie had been speared by a jolt of homesickness, but now wanted to respond to the hand that rested lightly between her shoulder blades—the man had no concept of personal body space. Unfortunately, as soon as he touched her everything, including her brain, refused to function. Actually, this was not totally correct; she could smell the soap he used mingled with other less familiar but not unpleasant male scents.

Luckily, the paralysis did not last more than a moment and Sophie didn't feel the inclination to examine the heart-racing breath-catching moment of paralysis too deeply.

It was obviously a postscript to her light-headed moment. Marco Speranza's physical presence was overwhelming and, standing beside him, crushingly devastating, but she wasn't going to faint just because he stood next to her.

She walked through the door into the outer office before him.

'Perhaps it would be better, Mr Speranza, if you let me explain things to Amber when I get back.' The man and woman who were sitting in the outer office looked up as they entered.

He angled a dark brow and echoed, 'Get back? Get back where?'

'Home…' She stopped abruptly, her face falling as she realised home was the one place she was not allowed to go. 'To London,' she added huskily.

Marco who had seen the flash of deep sadness on her face wondered what had put it there. Though, whatever personal problems this woman had they were none of his business unless they affected her work.

'I don't think, Miss Balfour, you understand that you have been on my payroll since we shook on this deal. I expect you to start work in the morning.'

CHAPTER SEVEN

SOPHIE stared at him in horror.

'Morning!' she yelped. 'But that's not possible. I'm only here for the night and I have nothing...' Literally nothing—unless the airline tracked down her lost luggage—not even a toothbrush. 'And we didn't shake.' It was not something she would have forgotten.

'You're a very literal-minded young woman,' Marco observed before adding, 'How young, really?'

'It's not polite to ask a woman's age, but I wasn't lying—I'm twenty-three.'

She lifted her chin and thought, *If he can ask so can I.* 'How old are you?'

'In experience, several centuries older than you, *cara.*'

His brow puckered as he studied her face. The exploits of the Balfour heiresses represented everything shallow and superficial that he had turned his back on after the divorce.

It remained a total mystery to him how a daughter of Oscar Balfour could utterly lack the glitter and polish that the Balfour name represented, how she could be so...wholesome and quite annoyingly naive.

The form of address brought a flush to Sophie's cheeks.

Marco saw the flush and produced a smile that did not warm his emerald eyes. 'The handshake can be remedied.'

Deeply regretting she had been so pedantic, Sophie viewed his extended hand with the sort of enthusiasm she'd had when she'd entered a gym at school.

'I trust you,' she said, tucking her hand behind her back.

A strangled sound from his subordinate drew Marco's attention to the couple at the desk.

'I might require you to work this weekend, Francesco.' He had the satisfaction of seeing the couple's faces drop in unison, as he stepped into the lift behind Sophie.

'Where are you staying?' He stopped beside a long sleek-looking convertible and opened the passenger door.

'I don't know—I came straight here from the airport. Amber hadn't booked anywhere as she was going to stay with a friend, but she said I should go to…' She reached into the capacious pocket of her loose-fitting jacket and withdrew the notepad inside, turning it to the relevant page.

She squeaked in protest as Marco plucked it from her fingers.

'A nice enough hotel,' he admitted. 'But you should stay at…'

The buzz in Sophie's head blocked the name. She had spent her life falling in with the suggestions made by others and felt a surge of uncharacteristic rebellion.

'Because you say so?'

Marco noted again that the beige English mouse looked decidedly more attractive with an antagonistic glitter in her wide-spaced, dramatically blue eyes.

She would also, he thought, look good in red.

It would bring out the creaminess in her skin tone… When was the last time he had seen a woman without any make-up?

'You would not find that argument compelling?'

'That wouldn't be an argument—that would be an order, Mr Speranza.' Something she was guessing he was rather good at doling out.

'Are you always so pedantic? And make it Marco.'

At one level Sophie knew that her gut reaction to the suggestion was disproportionate but she couldn't keep the horror from her voice as she said stiffly, 'I couldn't possibly.'

'Step outside your comfort zone, Sophie…' he goaded gently.

Her father had said exactly the same thing to her. Startled by the déjà vu, her eyes flew to his face… There was absolutely no resemblance between the man whose eyes connected with her own and Oscar Balfour.

She lowered her gaze and comforted herself with the thought that the opportunities to use his name were not going to be frequent.

Men like Marco Speranza delegated and she doubted he ever put himself in danger of getting a crease in his suit.

'I'm so far out of my comfort zone that I'm…' She stopped as a sudden ache of longing for the familiar things she had been forced to leave behind welled up inside her.

'You're what?'

'Fine, *Marco*,' she said, curling her tongue around his name with difficulty and trying not to think about the gatehouse.

'The hotel you speak of will be fully booked as they are hosting a convention. Most of the hotels in the city are full of people who like to dress up as aliens from film and TV.'

Sophie could see a flaw in his explanation. 'And the hotel you suggest won't be full?'

'I keep a suite there for business purposes. I'm quite happy to put it at your disposal.'

Business purposes. Was that a polite euphemism for love nest? Would she find a selection of sexy women's clothes in the wardrobes, silk sheets and champagne in the fridge? Her experience was limited, as in zero, and she found her sudden prurient interest in the subject troubling.

She gave a prim smile. 'I would not like to put you out,' she said, wondering if he ever double-booked the room.

While she was not addicted to the celebrity columns or, for that matter, the financial pages, she would have had to be living on another planet not to know that even though he had stepped off the celebrity-party circuit and gone reclusive he was rarely seen without female companionship.

It had crossed her mind that the beautiful trophy girlfriends might be a smokescreen—a way of hiding his broken heart from the world. Now having met him she felt it was more likely he just enjoyed shallow sex with beautiful women.

Marco looked amused. 'You can stop looking so alarmed, Miss Balfour. I am not inviting you to share my bed.'

The mortified colour flew to Sophie's cheeks. 'I never thought you were!' she choked.

Her emphatic response drew a curious look from him. 'Why not?'

Sure now that he was mocking her she shot him an unfriendly sideways look as he held open the passenger door for her.

She slid into the passenger seat. 'Men do not proposition me,' she said flatly.

Marco, his attention caught by the flash of something pale, glanced casually downwards. His drifting gaze stilled. Her skirt had bunched up and the paleness he saw was her thighs. They were rather superior thighs, as were the legs they were attached to, the sort of legs that most women would flaunt in short skirts and heels.

It was none of his business if Sophie Balfour chose to hide them under layers of unattractive clothes, but even a disinterested observer did have to wonder about this woman's hang-ups.

'But you would like them to? I suggest putting slightly more flesh on show.'

When the flesh in question was as good as hers it made sense.

His eyes drifted downwards once more; the milky paleness of her skin fascinated him.

Belatedly catching the direction of his stare Sophie twitched her rumpled skirt across her knees.

He returned her glare with a look that held no trace of embarrassment and suggested helpfully, 'Fewer layers, possibly.'

'Thank you for the fashion advice, but I would not like to be propositioned, especially by you.'

The horror in her voice brought a smile to his lips. 'Relax, you're safe from my attentions.'

Oh, yes. *I really needed that spelled out,* she thought, wondering what it would be like to *not* be *safe*… To actually be in danger because you aroused the predatory instincts of a man like Marco Speranza?

Her sisters, her beautiful Balfour siblings, would not be *safe* with Marco Speranza; he would not smirk at the thought of luring them to his love nest.

And when he lured, she was guessing not many girls resisted. Her glance brushed his wide mouth, and she thought maybe even fewer than not many. It was easy to see how a woman facing the prospect of being kissed by those lips might forget all about self-respect.

Sophie was very glad, having their best interests at heart, that her sisters were each safely tucked away miles from here. Marco Speranza was quite obviously a very dangerous man.

A man one woman had made a fool of, and he was now punishing the entire female race—or the drop-dead gorgeous ones anyway.

She was safe.

On that depressing note Sophie gave her head a shake to clear her thoughts and she schooled her features into an expression of mock horror. 'Oh, leave me my dreams,' she drawled.

She heard Marco chuckle as he walked around the car. 'You have a rich fantasy life, Sophie,' he observed, sliding in beside her.

He looked at her mouth and realised his own life was getting richer the longer he spent in this woman's company.

Sophie kept her eyes trained ahead as the door shut behind him, enclosing them in the luxurious air-conditioned leather-lined cocoon. The tension that she'd been holding in check, ever since she'd woken up and found herself being looked at by a pair of eyes as hard as emeralds, racked up another level.

Conscious that her heart was trying to batter its way through her ribcage, she lifted a hand to her throat and swallowed.

The combination of large man and enclosed space was claustrophobic; only she didn't suffer from claustrophobia—until now.

What I need is more breathing space, she thought, an open window. Breathe deep, she told herself, inhaling deeply and almost immediately regretting it. Her nostrils quivered.

The scent that hung around him was probably no different chemically speaking than the scent that came off any other clean warm male, except the undertones of spicy fragrance that made her nostrils flare was more expensive than one the average man in the street wore.

Sophie had no intention of looking at him. 'I'm far too busy for fantasies.'

'And too scared for reality?'

The sly suggestion sent the colour flying to her cheeks. Her decision not to look at him forgotten, she whipped around to glare at him.

'Look, I'm glad you're giving us the contract,' she admitted, her voice not quite as steady as she would have liked, but she was coherent which was good. 'But I think we should have some ground rules.'

His darkly defined brows lifted towards his ebony hairline. 'Do I have this right…? *You* want to set ground rules for *me*? I have to tell you that that is not *normally* the way it works.'

'I don't know how it works. I just know that…' She stopped because actually she didn't know much at all, certainly not why she felt it necessary to start this conversation in the first place.

Keeping her own counsel had always worked for her before.

He arched a questioning brow.

'Being my employer, which you're not because I work for Amber—'

'Because your father slept with her.'

'Being my employer,' she gritted doggedly, pursuing the thought to the end. 'Doesn't give you the right to…to…' Stamp around in my head with your size tens. 'Be personal.'

'You are a role model of professional detachment for us all.'

Sophie flashed him a look of seething dislike.

To her relief it did not take long to reach the hotel. Marco escorted her into the foyer where the decor matched the art-deco thirties architecture outside.

Marco watched her as she looked around; when she wasn't being guarded Sophie Balfour had one of the most expressive faces he had ever seen. For a woman who had presumably been raised in the lap of luxury she possessed an almost child-like appreciation. 'You approve?'

'It's really nice,' she said, her blue eyes glowing with pleasure as she examined the luxurious space. 'I'm a fan of art deco.'

'In its historical context,' he said with a cautionary note in his voice.

'Don't worry, I won't be tempted to install black PVC and leopard-skin prints in the bedrooms of your palazzo.'

He met her innocent look with a smile. 'I feel reassured. Luca will look after you,' he said, nodding in the direction of the dapper-looking suited figure who was approaching them. 'So try not to start a fight before I return.'

The charge startled Sophie. *'Me!'*

He smiled and looked more attractive and dangerous than in Sophie's opinion any man had a right to look.

Well, it had been quite an experience meeting Marco Speranza and seeing him smile, but it was one that she could put behind her now, which was just as well.

His personality was so overwhelming that it was hard to concentrate on anything else, and if she was to make a success of this job and prove herself—do her small part in retrieving the good name of the Balfours—she didn't need any distractions.

And Marco Speranza was a big distraction!

At the door he paused and turned back. Sophie, who was feeling dead on her feet, tensed.

'Be ready at eight…' He paused. She looked so small and utterly exhausted standing there that he adjusted his timetable. 'Be ready at eleven-thirty.' The decision had nothing to do with sympathy. It was purely practical; he needed her alert and functioning when he showed her what needed to be done.

'Eleven-thirty, of course,' Sophie said, hiding her relief as for a split second she had thought he had said eight.

'It is an hour's drive to the palazzo.'

'You're coming!' Sophie was startled; she had assumed that Marco Speranza would delegate such a task to one of his underlings, one that she had hoped would have a less deleterious effect on her nervous system.

'You look disappointed.'

'No, of course not,' Sophie denied unconvincingly.

'I would like to see your reaction to my home and hear your ideas.' He turned to the dapper-looking man, sliding seamlessly into Italian as they shook hands.

'Tell Luca if you need anything. I will see you in the morning, Sophia.' He tilted his head and moved away.

'Sophie,' she called after him, not liking the Latin treatment of her name—it implied an intimacy that didn't exist.

Marco didn't stop but turned his head to fling a grin at her over his shoulder.

The penthouse suite turned out to be just as luxurious as one might expect a suite Marco Speranza used to be, not that it bore any trace of his occupation. There were no slinky dresses in the wardrobes, but she was provided with a basket of all the essentials and a promise that her luggage would be there in the morning.

Sophie thought the promise was overly optimistic but, sure enough, when she woke up—she had fallen into a deep dreamless slumber almost before her head hit the pillow—someone who identified himself as a senior airport employee knocked on the door carrying her lost luggage.

His apologetic charm contrasted sharply with the brush off she'd received the previous day, but then she was sure that the name Marco Speranza worked miracles on Sicily.

She had just opened her cases when the text came from Amber. Sophie hadn't been sure how to tell her about Marco's choice. In the end, exhausted and fearing that she'd cave in a second if faced with Amber shrieking over the phone, she'd rung late last night and left a very short message. Amber's text was comprised mainly of excess punctuation and an order to *Sit tight, don't say anything more to him and I'll be there soon.* Knowing nothing she could say would prevent Amber's imminent arrival, Sophie headed downstairs.

The time was exactly eleven-thirty.

Marco was already sitting at a table with newspapers spread around him and a coffee in his hand.

He didn't immediately see her and Sophie had a chance to study his clear-cut classical profile. He really was good-looking enough to make a girl weep, and so rampantly male that it was no wonder a passing group of well-dressed women did everything but rip off their clothes to get his attention as they walked by, ogling him shamelessly.

Marco, his attention on the financial pages, appeared oblivious to the buzz of female interest.

Maybe he took it for granted? Maybe he took it as his due?

He still hadn't seen her and she was in no hurry to gain his attention. She felt pretty awkward about meeting him again after her performance the previous day.

She had lain in bed that morning reviewing the conversation, groaning at intervals as she recalled some of the things she had said to him.

Sophie had no idea what had come over her—she was always polite—but saw little point in stressing over this lapse, because it wasn't going to happen again.

She'd been tired and anxious and her emotions had been close to the surface. It had all got far too personal and she had been…well, she had been rude, and he had given her a contract. Sophie still hadn't quite got the why part straight in her head, but probably there was a lesson in that somewhere, though she wasn't sure what it was.

She had decided it was pointless to stress over yesterday; she needed to concentrate on today and the task ahead. Today would be different. Today she would keep things professional.

Marco glanced at his watch and went to fold one of the broadsheets spread before him and caught sight of her standing there.

'Good morning,' she said brightly.

He got to his feet and offered her coffee, which she refused. 'I've had breakfast.'

'I wasn't expecting to see you for a while yet,' he admitted.

Dressed today in faded denims that hinted at the muscles in his long powerful thighs and a plain white T-shirt, he was a much more relaxed-looking version of the Marco she had met the previous day.

More relaxed but still devastatingly attractive. Italian men wore clothes well.

'You did say eleven-thirty, didn't you?'

'I did but you looked tired enough to sleep the clock around last night.'

Having been shocked by the haggard face that had looked back at her from a mirror illuminated by unforgiving lights Sophie was well aware what she had looked like last night.

She met his eyes levelly, aware that the gentle buzz of the

room had receded. It was as if when he was around there was no room in her head for anyone else.

She pushed aside the whimsical thought.

'It had been a long day, but I'm fine now. I even had my own toothbrush this morning and my own clothes. I can't believe they found my baggage so quickly.'

Marco's brows lifted as he agreed. 'Amazing.'

'I don't suppose you'd know anything about that?'

His look of innocent bewilderment was so phoney that despite herself she laughed. 'Well, I'm grateful and terribly impressed by your influence.'

'I would have thought it would take more than that to impress a Balfour girl.' He saw her flinch and wondered what nerve he'd touched.

'The name is Sophie,' she said flatly. Unable to stop herself she added, 'Did you give me the contract because I'm a Balfour?'

She waited tensely for his response; it would not exactly be the first time someone had cultivated her because they wanted access to her father or a date with one of her sisters.

And this was something she wanted on her own merits; until this moment she hadn't known how much getting it with no string pulling meant to her. The success would have no meaning if she discovered it was the Balfour brand and not her talent that had swung the deal.

Marco, who had also been born with a name that made people assume things before they met him, understood what she was saying. 'No, I gave it to you *despite* your name.'

Sophie's startled eyes flew to his face. '*Despite.*'

He said nothing, just slung her an enigmatic look, his eyes glittering and hard, from under his dark brows and extended his arm, inviting her to walk beside him.

She knew eyes followed their progress towards the exit and wondered if the people watching had seen the danger in him too.

Some people were attracted by danger; she was glad she was not one of them.

Marco led her to a long low chauffeur-driven limousine, explaining his choice of transport by saying he had work to do.

Just as Sophie was about to step inside, a series of loud squeals and her name being called stopped her. She turned and her heart dropped. Too late. Sukie and Emma were running as fast as their high heels would take them along the pavement towards her.

Marco angled a brow. 'Friends?'

Sophie struggled to adopt a philosophical attitude to the fact her big break was about to come to an abrupt end and shook her head. 'Colleagues,' she said, reminding herself she hadn't even wanted the job anyway…which begged the question, why did she feel like a kid who had just had her favourite teddy bear snatched away?

Sukie reached her first. 'Sophie, we've been looking for you everywhere, poor darling. You look exhausted, doesn't she, Emma?' Sukie said, patting her hand absently as she gazed up at Marco, fluttering her lashes so hard Sophie was surprised they didn't come unglued.

'Poor Sophie. Never mind—you can sleep on the flight home,' Emma said, extending her hand to Marco breathlessly. 'The office sent us to take over, Mr Speranza…Marco…'

Marco didn't take the hand. 'Then you had a wasted journey, ladies. I have my team leader.'

Sukie's glance shifted to Sophie. 'Sophie.'

She exchanged a bewildered look with Emma, who said, 'But that's Sophie.'

'I know who she is. You, however, I do not know.' His expression as he nodded dismissal suggested he did not wish to. 'Good morning, ladies. Sophie?'

Obeying the pressure of the hand on her shoulder Sophie got into the limo. She turned her head as they drew away, knowing she would always cherish the expressions on the two girls' faces.

Aware that Marco's eyes were on her face she turned back. 'You were awfully rude to them. Did you see their faces when… I think I enjoyed it.' Sophie gave a shamefaced grin and asked worriedly, 'Does that make me a terrible person?'

'Are they always that dismissive of you?' Having seen how sharp her tongue was it bewildered him that Sophie let them get away with it. 'If you think I was being *awfully rude* to them, then it appears your education has been sadly neglected.'

'Working for you will probably fill in the gaps,' she retorted, then amazed by her own daring she lapsed into silence.

And so did Marco, as after the car had pulled smoothly away he opened a laptop.

Half an hour later, she looked at his dark head, bent over the screen, with a certain resentment; his concentration was total, but his manners were appalling.

It wasn't that she wanted to chat but having her presence acknowledged would be nice.

Lips compressed into a thin disapproving line, she fished into her bag and extracted the guidebook she had picked up in the hotel that morning. Consulting the map in the centre pages, she attempted to match it to the scenery they were passing through and tried to work out what route they were taking.

It was hard to figure out because she hadn't noticed what route they had used when they left Palermo; she had been too busy admiring the incredible mixture of architecture the city offered, from Byzantine to Norman. Some areas were run-down and dilapidated, some grand. Palermo was a cultural and architectural melting pot, and one that boasted more crazy drivers a square mile than any place she had ever been.

Sophie was about to give up on the impossible task of figuring out where they were when Marco sighed, leaned across and took the book from her hands.

Sophie glared and lifted her chin. 'Do you mind?'

'We are,' he said, handing the book back to her, 'here.' He

pressed his thumb against a spot on the map, then moved it to another spot, adding, 'And we are heading there.' His attention shifted to her face. She was relieved he did not comment on her flushed cheeks. If she leaned a little closer their shoulders would be touching...

'I am not ignoring you... All right,' he conceded, anticipating her protest, 'I am, but I do have work to do, so stop attention seeking. Your fidgeting is distracting!'

So was the scent of her newly washed hair which had already mostly escaped the ponytail she had secured it in. Curling fronds framed her face, giving her an angelic look that was at stark variance with the evil look she was giving him.

'I am not attention seeking!' Her indignation was not feigned—of all the things he could have accused her of this was the most unfair!

He ignored the protest and directed his gaze through the window. 'This area is a nature reserve, *parco naturale*. The mountain range is the Madonie. I think you'll find the rest of the guidebook drivel on page six.

'Now try, if you can, to amuse yourself. *Dio mio!* If I had known I was travelling with a six-year-old I would have brought crayons and colouring books.'

Sophie's murderous glare was utterly wasted as he had tuned her out again. 'Do you work at being offensive?'

'Not any longer. I perfected the art years ago.'

'Well, that's not something to be proud of,' she heard herself observe.

He closed the computer and put it to one side with a long-suffering sigh. 'You win. You have me.'

'I don't want you.' Now that, she thought, could not be something he heard every day.

'I'll only make such an offer once...' he taunted, trying to figure what it was about this small English woman that ate away at his patience.

She seemed to him like a woman half alive and yet there was all that passion just below the surface… He concluded it was the wasteful nature of this situation; she had life, something many people fought tooth and nail for, and she was not living it.

If there was a man in her life he clearly wasn't doing his job properly.

Sophie let out a small shriek and grabbed the seat to steady herself as the limo rounded a sharp bend. If she loosened her grip she was going to slide into him.

So don't loosen!

'I'm quite happy with my guidebook,' she said, trying not to see herself pressed up close to him. 'And it's a lot more…' Her voice faded as she saw his arms closing around her, drawing her…

'We're here.'

She expelled a shaky sigh and pushed free of the shameful earthy images in her head. Then she saw where she would be working. 'Oh, my goodness! How beautiful!' she gasped.

Sophie had not exactly been brought up in a shoe box herself; she was used to luxury, but this was on another scale. No wonder Amber wanted this contract so much, she mused.

'Renaissance?' She flashed him a questioning look and saw he was watching her. The enigmatic expression in his deep-set eyes made her shiver and look away.

Marco nodded. 'The facade is, but some parts date from a much earlier period. Some people believe that…'

Sophie was interested—she really was—but she struggled to concentrate on what he was saying. His words seemed somehow passionless in comparison to the beauty of the building. All she wanted to do was escape this wretched car and his disturbingly close proximity and explore.

'Are you all right?'

'Fine!' Sophie tugged fretfully at the neck of her top. She really needed to cool off before she made a total fool of herself.

'I thought I'd let you get the feel of the place alone.'

Sophie, who had seconds before been wishing him a million miles away, found her reaction to the news that her wish had been partially granted worryingly ambiguous.

'Good idea.'

The door opened and she tumbled out. Having filled her lungs with pine-scented air she turned her attention to the palazzo. It was breathtaking. The only palazzo she'd seen on the journey here had been crumbling, and this certainly wasn't; although for all its magnificence it did have an unloved look to it.

'How many rooms are there?' she asked, thinking she could easily get lost.

'I have never counted. Ah, here they are.'

Sophie watched as Marco greet the elderly couple who were walking towards them. He shook hands with the man and hugged the woman, who to Sophie's amazement ruffled his hair. The affection between them was obvious.

'This is Alberto and Natalia.' Marco's smile was warm and carried no hidden agenda.

'They,' he said, 'are here if you need them. This is Miss Balfour.'

'Sophie,' she corrected him, smiling at the couple, the man lean and angular, the woman soft and round.

'I will see you later and you can tell me what you are going to do to bring our palazzo back to life.'

She wrinkled her nose at his choice of words. 'It doesn't look dead to me.'

'Looks can be deceptive, *cara*. Its heart,' he said clamping a hand to his own chest, 'is quite dead.' And a man could walk and talk, function, even laugh, and be quite dead at his heart.

Sophie was still puzzling over this extraordinary statement when he strode away without a backward glance. Marco Speranza, with his combustible combination of Sicilian pride and passion, was a deeply troubling man. Or was that troubled? she wondered.

Marco's home was an incredible building, filled with treasures that one rarely saw outside a museum. In fact, the place reminded Sophie more of a museum—the old-fashioned musty variety—than a home, and there was a pervasive air of neglect that was dispiriting.

Sophie tried to be tactful, but when faced with a bucket situated below a dark stain in the ceiling she could not hide her disapproval.

'One storm and that whole ceiling will be down!'

The upkeep on a place like this might be a financial burden for some but not Marco.

'It was not always like this, but since the divorce he could not bear to come here. She was a bad one, the one he married. There were men,' Natalia told her darkly. 'Many men and drink and still the *marchese* let her do anything she wanted.'

'*Marchese?*'

The older woman shrugged and gave a puzzled frown. 'Of course, there was no other son, or daughter—it is very sad. This place needs the sound of children's laughter. Are you perhaps…?' She looked Sophie up and down as though assessing her child-bearing hip potential.

Sophie gave a strained laugh. 'Good God, no, I'm just here to decorate.'

'You don't like children either?'

'I love children but not here…his…' She trailed off. How did she explain to this nice woman that the man she clearly adored did not date women who looked like her? Instead she turned the subject to the painting behind her that looked suspiciously like a Titian.

As she wandered later through the warren of rooms upstairs Sophie's thoughts returned to this extraordinary conversation. It was very hard to imagine the arrogant, proud man she had met allowing his wife to humiliate him.

It seemed safe to assume that Marco must have been totally besotted with Allegra to put up with it, but finally she had pushed him too far.

CHAPTER EIGHT

MARCO spent several hours with his estate manager, Juan. Horseback was still the best way to explore the more inaccessible corners of the sprawling Speranza estate and together he and Juan rode to the area of ancient woodland, some of which Juan had suggested it would be more profitable to fell.

'I have the figures and it really does look like a no-brainer. We could cut a road straight through to the vineyards—it would save miles—and we could plant…'

Marco, riding a few feet ahead, listened to the enthusiastic plans in silence. Sophie Balfour's face, her blue eyes raised in reverential awe to the palazzo, kept flashing into his head at intervals.

The intervals were getting shorter.

It was inexplicable. What was it about this girl—for no one could call her a woman—that dominated his thoughts?

She was far from the type of woman he went for. Sophie Balfour was high maintenance…yet… Was he attracted to her?

*Well, if you don't know…*Marco mocked the voice in his head.

They reached a point where the trees cleared and the ground fell away to a sheer precipice that gave a view all the way to the sea in the west.

'I can let you have the figures…'

Marco tore his eyes from the view. 'That won't be necessary.'

The other man smiled in satisfaction. 'Then can I set things in motion?'

'No. I'm sure your figures add up and it makes financial sense, but this land…' He breathed deeply, inhaling the forest air, as his eyes swept the breathtaking vista before them. 'It is not all about balance sheets. I do not wish to stand here one day and describe to my children what the ancient Nebrodi fir once looked like.'

Always supposing he had children.

The manager looked disappointed but recognised defeat in his employer's non-negotiable tone and a change of mood in his stony set expression.

He gave a philosophical shrug and suggested that Marco might like to see the progress they had made with the marsh area that had been set aside for conservation.

Marco, already wheeling his mount around, shook his head. 'No, I must get back.'

There was a brooding expression on Marco's lean face as he left the stables and re-entered the palazzo. There was no sign of Sophie. He walked from room to room, calling her name and getting increasingly irritated when there was no response.

Speaking to Juan of continuity and family had resurrected memories that were even now raw and humiliating.

He stood at the bottom of the sweeping marble staircase that Allegra had had wanted covered in gold leaf and bellowed, 'Sophie!' He paused, waiting. Again there was no response. 'This is what you get when you employ amateurs.' And this, he thought, looking around his unloved home, is what you get when you're young and idealistic and you equate great sex with love and get married.

When he had married, Marco had seen his future stretching ahead. A future that included children and growing old with his soulmate.

His bride had shared his dreams, at least until the ring was on her finger. Then Allegra had admitted she had other plans, and those plans did not include children or growing old.

The look of revulsion on her beautiful face when he had brought up the subject of children and the incredulity in her laughter as she had dismissed the idea were etched like acid into his mind.

'Children would *ruin* my figure…you wouldn't want a fat and ugly wife, would you, Marco?' The idea of children was as repugnant to her as the suggestion of a line on her beautiful face.

Still he hadn't understood. Blinkers firmly in place, he'd thought that all Allegra needed was reassurance that he would still love her.

It was three months later that the scales finally fell from his eyes, three months later when she had had her first affair and laughed and not even attempted to deny it when he challenged her with his discovery.

'You were away and I was bored. What are you going to do, Marco, divorce me?' She had smiled complacently at her reflection in the mirror. 'But you won't, will you,' she said, her eyes mocking him, scanning his face to watch her words hit home. 'Because that isn't the Sicilian way, not the *Speranza* way. You are as romantic and foolish as your father with his ideals! And where did ideals get him? Who cares now what he stood for? He died, and all his pointless principles went with him.'

Marco had not given her the satisfaction of seeing how much her vicious words had hurt. His only defence was to have none, to remain unmoved. He had hidden his feelings but Allegra had never stopped trying. She got some sort of sick kick from turning the knife, pushing him, waiting for him to finally snap.

The woman he had married had been the ultimate hedonist, who had only ever loved the things the Speranza money and name could buy, including fame, which she craved like a drug.

Reaching the top of the staircase Marco took a deep breath

and closed a mental door on the bitter memories. The man he had been then was long dead.

He paused, calling out once more as he decided which direction to take.

Where was the woman?

He began a systematic search of the west wing, about to take a left turn when the sound of a distant voice made Marco veer right. Who was she talking to?

'Oh, my goodness!'

The exclamation drew Marco to the open door of one of the rooms to his left.

He pushed open the door and stepped inside, mentally preparing himself for the sensory assault of the utterly inappropriate hand-painted black Chinese silk wallpaper that he knew covered the ancient stone walls. Added to the vast waterbed that took pride of place, this shrine to bad taste had been Allegra's room.

Her back turned to him, Sophie Balfour was standing by the bed, her head tilted back and her eyes trained on the mirrored ceiling above it.

He had forgotten the mirror and, until this moment, Allegra's spiteful drunken taunts of the sexual romps she had enjoyed with his best friend in this bed. Not the best of memories but actually not the worst either. By this point in their train wreck of a marriage his ex-wife had no longer had the power to hurt him, only to disgust him.

'Oh, my goodness!'

The exclamation, hushed and shaky this time, brought his attention back to the figure by the bed. The memories that filled his mouth with a sour taste vanished and Marco was forced to bite back a laugh.

He had never thought he'd laugh in this room.

Guilt and curiosity warred on Sophie's face as she pressed the mattress, then sprang back when it quivered.

Standing in the shadows Marco heard her tell herself, 'You have led a very sheltered life, Sophie Balfour.'

He was inclined to agree with this assessment, though not being as ignorant of her family history—at least, some of the recent parts—as he had allowed her to think he found this circumstance nothing short of amazing.

Part of him had clung to the belief that the wholesome innocence thing was part of an act, but nobody, he realised now, was that good an actress.

As he watched, she reached out and touched the bed with her hand, in doing so turning a little so that she presented her profile rather than her back to him. At some point since they had parted she had gathered her hair into a haphazard knot on the back of her head, dragging it from her face and revealing a profile that was classically pure.

But it was not her face that Marco's eyes were glued to; it was her body, for her hair was not the only change. The mushroom-coloured shirt that had enveloped her diminutive frame from shoulder to knee was gone.

The jeans underneath were utilitarian rather than fashionable and were also ill fitting—no surprise there. The surprise was that Sophie Balfour had a waist, and one that he could have spanned with his hands.

Had Marco felt inclined to mix business with pleasure it would be a pleasure to explore that body, because if the waist had been a shock the rest of her was a total and utter jaw-dropping revelation. Under her tent-like uniforms his interior designer had been hiding a body that invited sinful speculation.

An hourglass that would put any pin-up to shame. Below the tiny waist her hips flared full and feminine, and above… A silent sigh locked in his throat as his hot gaze moved over the outline of her full breasts, revealed in a skimpy vest affair that left very little to the imagination.

Despite this, his imagination remained active.

His fingers flexed and he felt the gush of hot desire tighten in his belly, as in his mind he traced a path over that soft warm skin and sensuous inviting curves.

And why resist the invitation they offered? he asked himself. Why rule out the possibility of enjoying that warm, womanly invitation?

Why?

There was shock in his shadowed emerald eyes as he shook his head, a hard ironic smile of self-mockery tugging the corners of his sensual mouth upwards as he followed her actions with his eyes. Still oblivious to his presence, she angled another guilty glance at the ceiling.

Why?

Why not mix business with pleasure? Why become involved with a woman—no, a *girl*—who probably still believes in the Easter bunny and true love and blushes like a virgin?

That he had been tempted, however briefly, meant he was clearly losing his mind. Mental note, Marco, make more time in your schedule for sex with a woman who understood that sex was physical not spiritual, a pleasure enjoyed and walked away from.

Sophie Balfour, who could only show passion for a colour chart, was clearly not such a woman, though she equally clearly had potential.

It was that potential, that inner untapped core of passion he had glimpsed in her, that had both tempted him and swung his decision.

A man who did ignite the dormant passion that smouldered in those big blue eyes might consider the inevitable complications worth it… He was not such a man.

He turned, his intention to walk away unseen, when she gave a deep little laugh. The husky sound had an earthy tactile quality that stopped Marco in his tracks.

As he watched, her body language changed to a combination of defiance and mischief. She kicked off her shoes and crawled into the middle of the bed before stretching out on her back. Then, as though overcome by the sheer audacity of her actions, she lay there staring at her reflection, her ribcage rising and falling in tune to the rapid breaths that pushed her breasts against the stretchy fabric of her vest.

There was an illicit thrill about lying here in the bed, but the thrill soured when she realised that Marco might have shared it with his beautiful ex-wife.

Her heart beat hard against her breastbone as she lay there, not seeing her own tangled fair hair spread against the black silk, but rich raven lustrous coils spread on the pillow. The two figures, their bodies, one slim, pale and perfect, one golden and hard as coiled steel, were sinuously entwined. It was so real that she could almost hear the gasps of their shared passion.

She pressed a hand to her mouth as the taste of acid rose in her throat.

Did he still love his beautiful wife despite what she had done? Would he have taken her back had his pride allowed it?

It would take a woman like one of the stunning Balfour girls to make him forget that amazing siren, and in the meantime he clearly intended working his way through every beautiful woman that appeared on his radar.

But being a Balfour girl in name only she was safe. She was minus the charm and confidence and drop-dead gorgeous looks; she just had the name, which impressed him not at all.

In some ways this was a plus point; he didn't have a preconceived expectation of what she *ought* to be had the gene pool not decided to have a little joke at her expense. It was liberating not to be crushingly conscious of her Balfour legacy all the time. And as she didn't want to impress, except in the professional sense...

Of course, not wanting to impress him did not stop her wistfully wondering what it would be like to have the ability to bedazzle him and make him laugh. Her chest hurt; feelings she did not want to own up to were locked like a tight fist at the base of her throat.

Jolted from her miserable reflections by the sudden movement of the bed, Sophie's hand fell away and her eye-lashes lifted from her cheeks.

The picture in the mirror now reflected the one in her head with a couple of significant differences—the woman wasn't beautiful and Marco was wearing clothes.

Clothes or not, the real man was a lot harder for her out-of-control hormones to cope with than the imaginary naked image.

Sophie realised she was staring and had been for God knows how long. She tore her eyes away at once. Anything would be preferable to him guessing his plain-Jane decorator was lusting after him. She struggled inelegantly to rise.

'I'm sorry I just…'

A finger against her breastbone sent her back into the gently undulating mattress.

The finger stayed there and Marco, who had rolled onto his side, showed no immediate sign of removing it as he levelled an emerald-eyed stare at her face.

He seemed comfortable with the silence and the physical contact. Sophie was not.

'Now this is extremely…not normal. I wasn't sleeping in your bed. It was research… I've never tried out a waterbed… I've not tried out a lot of things…' She compressed her lips to forestall further unnecessary confessions on this subject and added huskily. 'It's weird.'

'The bed?'

She shook her head. 'No, though that,' she admitted, patting it and giving a nervous laugh, 'is weird too. You're going to ask me weird good or weird bad.' He's going to ask you to shut up, Sophie, so why don't you? 'The jury is still out,' she admitted, drawing breath before returning to her original theme. 'Haven't you ever noticed people are divided into talkers and listeners? I'm a listener—I talk very little. I'm renowned for my reserve, did you know that? Of course you didn't, but since I got here I can't seem to stop talking.'

Her eyes widened as a finger was placed on her lips. 'Take a deep breath and relax.'

'I am relaxed.'

'You're hyperventilating. You were curious, I understand that! Sexual curiosity is what makes the world go around.'

'If you say so… I mean, mirrors and waterbeds may be your thing but for me they're pretty much…'

Her eyes connected with his, and a whoosh of heat crackled through her body.

'This isn't my bed, *cara*.'

'It…' She stopped her brows drawing together in a disconcerted frown as she pulled herself into a sitting position. 'What did you just call me?'

Lying on his back Marco tucked one hand behind his head and looked up at her. Her heart stumbled and skipped a beat as his eyes brushed her own before sliding down her body. 'My imagination does not require props.' It required a leash! Just looking at that creamy skin made him want to bury his face in her softness and taste all that sinfully tempting sweetness.

Feeling several hundred degrees hotter than she had when she had removed her outer layers to cool off Sophie looked around frantically for something to cover herself.

'It's warm, and I was…'

'Relax.'

She dragged her eyes from his mouth and got as far as his shadowed jaw.

'I am relaxed!' she heard herself bellow defiantly. 'Totally relaxed.'

'Good…no, don't move yet.' He didn't catch her arm but his fingers grazed it; her skin was so sensitized that her nerve endings reacted to the movement of air. 'This is comfortable.' He flexed his shoulders.

Sophie, who felt ready to crawl out of her skin, gave a grunt that could at a push have passed as agreement.

'I haven't been in the saddle for a month and I'm feeling it.'

He would look good on a horse. He would look good on pretty much anything. 'If you're stiff you should take a hot bath.'

'I thought it was a cold shower?'

That was it; she was out of here. His earthy laughter ringing in her ears, she tumbled out—elegance was not an option—of the waterbed.

Marco followed suit and stood there, dragging a hand through his dark hair.

Sophie rounded on him. 'I suppose you think that was funny.'

Bosom heaving, creamy satiny skin, freckles, flashing eyes and *that mouth*—the woman was killing him. 'I simply mean that there is no hot water at the moment as we have a plumbing situation.'

Sophie said, 'Oh!' and felt stupid.

'How did your exploration go? Do you have any questions?'

'Yes,' Sophie admitted, thinking, Do you still love your wife?

'I need to know just how far you want me to go….' She closed her eyes as the mortified colour rushed to her cheeks; she couldn't seem to open her mouth without a double entendre escaping. 'With the palazzo, I mean. Do I need to run every idea by you or…?'

'I am totally in your hands, *cara*.'

His mockery stung. Did he think that just because she was plain and plump and probably didn't even register a blip on his chart of female and desirable that she didn't have feelings?

His smile faded, leaving in its place an expression nothing like mockery, an expression that sent her sensitive stomach into a spiralling dive.

'You're a very attractive woman.'

It was an accusation and one she didn't know how to respond to.

'I mention this because you're going to be living under this roof while the place is filled with workmen—Italian workmen, Sicilian workmen—who need little encouragement.'

Having delivered this lecture he turned abruptly and walked out of the room, leaving her staring in bewilderment after him.

CHAPTER NINE

SOPHIE listened quietly, betraying no emotion while the man spoke, stabbing the air with an accusing finger towards her, as his attack grew more overtly personal.

Very aware of the eyes watching, though not of the pair of green ones that observed from the shadows, Sophie took a deep breath. She knew that if she did not establish her authority now she never would.

Since day one Franco's resentment at being answerable to a woman and one who was young had been obvious. He made no secret of the fact that he thought he ought to be managing the project and he had lost no opportunity to undermine her, constantly questioning her decisions and making snide references to her lack of experience.

Sophie had tried to ignore him and she had tried to placate him; neither strategy had worked. Now it was crunch time.

'I always appreciate your advice, Franco, but Roman is right.' She glanced with a smile towards the gangly young man whose adherence to her instructions had made things kick off on this occasion. He stood in front of the partially exposed fresco as though he were willing to physically defend it from attack. 'Thanks, Roman,' she added. 'But why don't you take your break now.'

Waiting until the reluctant, protective youth had moved away she turned back to the angry older man and smiled. She pitched her voice low, but loud enough for the men in the farthest corners of the room to hear, as she added calmly, 'I did tell Roman that we are stripping back this area by hand. I know it will take longer,' she added before the older man could interrupt. 'But restoration,' she added quietly, 'as I'm sure you'd agree, is about preserving when possible and not destroying. And this fresco—' she pointed to the area where the warm, amazingly vibrant colours had been revealed when the layer of crumbling plaster had fallen away that morning '—is something we have a duty to preserve.'

The older man flushed with displeasure and took a swaggering step towards her. 'The *marchese* will not weep when he sees it and it is his money you are wasting…'

Sophie's chin went up another notch at the scornful reminder to her own reaction when the hidden treasure had been revealed. She was not in the least ashamed of her emotional response.

'The *marchese* has put me in charge, Franco, and I know he hopes we can work together. He values your experience as much as I do.'

In the shadows, his hands clenched into fists at his sides, Marco was torn between a desire to applaud Sophie's sheer guts as she held her ground and his urge to strangle the truculent man he was apparently meant to value so highly.

Sophie Balfour had a quiet dignity that you couldn't teach— God, she had guts—and she looked so damned small with that beefy bear of a guy standing over her that he had to fight down the urge that made him want to rush in and rescue her.

She wouldn't thank him and she would be right; he knew he wouldn't be doing her any favours and that this was one battle she had to fight alone, but this knowledge didn't stop him wanting to rip her persecutor limb from limb.

He never had any time for men who felt threatened by capable women, and Sophie Balfour wasn't just capable, she was magnificent! And the jeans and T-shirt look suited her, he decided, feeling the usual kick of lust as his eyes slid with slow appreciation over her heavenly curves.

Sophie's steady blue gaze locked onto the older man's dark angry glare as she dropped her voice to a level intended for his ears alone. 'I would regret it if we could not work harmoniously together on this,' Sophie said, and she paused to let her words sink in. 'I'll make mistakes,' she conceded. 'And I hope I'll learn from them, but I'll definitely take responsibility for them, because that's what being the *boss* is about.' The emphasis was slight but she knew he picked it up. 'Now about the problem with the electrical contractors, do you think we should…?' She turned and after a pause Franco followed her.

Ten minutes later Sophie sank down under a giant oak tree and, head on her trembling knees, expelled a long, shaky breath. Her heart was still pounding like a piston.

'I called myself the boss.' She covered her face with her hands and began to laugh. 'Wait until I tell Mia.' Mia of all her sisters would appreciate the joke.

'Who is Mia?'

'My sister…' Sophie stopped, her blue eyes flying upwards to the tall man who had materialised out of nowhere. 'You, here…? I…' She started to rise, then stopped, sinking with a bump to the ground as Marco dropped down, balancing with casual grace on his heels.

Had Franco already taken his complaints to the top? Had Marco come to put her in her place and tell her she was doing everything wrong?

'How are things going?'

A casually innocent comment?

Or a leading question?

Sophie, lifting a hand to shade her eyes from the sun's glare, regarded his dark handsome face warily. She found it hard to associate anything innocent with someone who possessed a mouth that sinfully sexual. She pressed her back into the tree bark as a shiver traced a sensuous path down her spine.

'No problems?' His eyes drifted downwards, attracted by the hint of creamy cleavage and freckles; he wondered if she was wearing sunscreen to protect that glorious satiny skin.

Why, are you thinking of offering to put some on, Marco?

'What sort of problems?'

'Industrial unrest?' he said, seeing his finger slide into the shadowy valley between her breasts.

Her eyes flew wide—he knew!

Marco's jaw clenched and the muscles in his throat worked as he wrenched his gaze upwards and loosened his tie. 'You handled that very well back there.'

This time it was Sophie's mouth that gaped as she scrambled to her feet, shaking. 'You saw, you heard...'

'*You* conquered,' he inserted, rising with languid grace to his feet to tower over her. 'Your father would have been proud.'

Are you? Sophie only just managed to bite back the response. Why would his opinion matter more to her than that of her father?

'Do you want me to sack him?'

The casual offer made her stare, horrified. 'You can't just sack people!'

'Isn't that what you just threatened to do in so many words?'

'Then the hiring and firing really is up to me?' Then frightened that question made her sound like some sort of power-hungry megalomaniac she added quickly, 'Not that I would.'

'You're the boss.' He placed a hand on the broad tree trunk behind her head. 'And I think you like it.'

Sophie froze, a tiny choked sound escaping her aching throat as Marco leaned into her; at no point did their bodies touch but the idea was there in her head—*touch me, touch me!*

The idea, combined with the heat coming from his lean body and the scent of the cologne he used mixed with the underlying musky male scent of his skin, had a narcotic quality.

It struck a dazed and breathless Sophie that if anyone had seen them from a distance they might have looked like lovers, and having the men think she slept her way into the job would hardly help her credibility.

Might be worth it, though, mused the shameless voice in her head.

'You think I like being the boss…?' she echoed, struggling to sound normal and dispassionately curious and sounding anything but.

'It's good to be in…control,' Marco said, unable to recall the last time he had felt so little in control, certainly of his physical appetites. What was it about this woman that bypassed his brain and tapped into emotions he had put into cold storage years ago? He thought of the rush of pleasure he had felt as he drew up into the forecourt earlier, of the ferocious anger he had felt towards Franco mere moments ago. How long had it been since he had felt so at prey to his changing emotions? So…alive?

What was it that he actually wanted?

He did not trust his feelings, and he tried not to trust her…but he did! That was the problem. She looked at him with those big blue eyes and he lost all objectivity. He had wanted to rip that man into pieces just for being mean to her.

Sophie had to grab the tree to stop her knees folding when without warning he straightened up and stepped back, dragging a hand through his dark hair as he did so. His eyes were suddenly as cool as his manner.

'Do not let anyone touch the fresco until I've contacted an expert.'

Sophie's head was still spinning at the sudden change in emotional temperature; clearly, the erotic moment had only existed within her overheated imagination.

She felt the heat climb to her cheeks as she made herself meet his clinical gaze.

Marco Speranza being attracted to me…sure, that's so

likely. In future she decided she would keep her fantasies firmly under control.

'I have already rung the museum. They're sending someone tomorrow morning to advise.'

He raised a brow. 'You will let me know what they decide?'

She inclined her head and tried to match his bewilderingly chilly, formal manner as she had promised herself she would.

The man, she decided as she watched him walk away, was too moody for comfort. One minute she felt able to say anything to him and the next he was aloof and standoffish. And he hadn't, she realised, even said why he was there to begin with.

'Did you have something in particular to…?' she began, raising her voice.

He turned at the sound of her voice, pinning her with a glittering emerald stare and making Sophie lose her train of thought.

'It might be better if you commuted.'

The abrupt change of subject made her blink.

'The conditions here are…primitive,' he said, thinking he could not be the only male who had noticed how attractively she filled out jeans and a T-shirt.

'I like it here! It's convenient.'

Studying her mulish expression in silence for a moment, he shrugged. 'As you wish. I will be back tomorrow to speak with the experts from the museum.'

Sophie was unable to hide her dismay at the prospect. 'You will?'

'I am free.'

Sophie managed a weak smile. 'That's…great.'

It was after midnight when the last kinks were finally smoothed from the contract, the *T*'s crossed and the *I*'s dotted. The deal was finally, successfully completed and Marco could shrug off his jacket, the success all the more sweet because popular and informed opinion had called it impossible.

GET 2 BOOKS

We'd like to send you two *Harlequin Presents®* novels absolutely free.
Accepting them puts you under no obligation to purchase any more books.

HOW TO GET YOUR
2 FREE BOOKS AND 2 FREE GIFTS

1. Return the reply card today, and we'll send you two *Harlequin Presents* novels, absolutely free! We'll even pay the postage!

2. Accepting free books places you under no obligation to buy anything, ever. Whatever you decide, the free books and gifts are yours to keep, free!

3. We hope that after receiving your free books you'll want to remain a subscriber, but the choice is yours—to continue or cancel, any time at all!

EXTRA BONUS

You'll also get two free mystery gifts! (worth about $10)

FREE!

Return this card promptly to get
2 FREE BOOKS and 2 FREE GIFTS!

◆ HARLEQUIN®

Presents

YES! Please send me 2 FREE *Harlequin Presents*®
novels, and 2 free mystery gifts as well. I understand
I am under no obligation to purchase anything, as
explained on the back of this insert.

*About how many NEW paperback fiction books have
you purchased in the past 3 months?*

❏ 0-2   ❏ 3-6   ❏ 7 or more
E9K7   E9LK   E9LV

❏ I prefer the regular-print edition   ❏ I prefer the larger-print edition
    106/306 HDL   176/376 HDL

FIRST NAME

LAST NAME

ADDRESS

APT.#	CITY

STATE/PROV.	ZIP/POSTAL CODE

Visit us at:
www.ReaderService.com

It was almost 1:00 a.m. when Marco stepped into the glass elevator.

His team, all on an ebullient high, had already left. He assumed they were heading towards a fashionable nightspot to celebrate. They had invited him, of course, safe in the knowledge that he would refuse.

Marco shared their adrenaline buzz, but company and bright lights were not things he sought at such times; they were things he actively avoided. His tastes and pleasures were simpler— the privacy of his own apartment, his favourite jazz playing and perhaps a glass of brandy were the things he anticipated with pleasure as he drove through the city.

Strange then that when he came to the junction that led to his apartment he carried on driving.

He told himself that it would take him another hour before he reached the palazzo and that it would no doubt be in darkness. However, he continued to drive, deliberately not thinking about the impulse that made him do so until he reached the newly reinstated gated entrance to the estate.

The work was three weeks in now and it was going well. Sophie knew the timescale down to the nearest minute; it was one of many details circulating in her overactive brain. She had been terrified that the sheer size of this project would overwhelm her, but juggling information, tasks, times and dates was actually, she had discovered, quite a buzz.

So was the fact that she was good at it.

The ballroom had been the biggest job they faced, but well worth the effort, and what the painstaking process of removing layers of paint and grime had revealed was better than anyone, including the stonemasons, had anticipated.

There were only two places where the original stucco needed replacing.

Sophie had used every suitable Italian word of praise for the team of stonemasons who had worked diligently. Now, as she lay on her back on top of the scaffold tower, she knew they had deserved all of them and more.

Sophie shone her torch at the newly revealed relief work. Standing below, the craftsmanship of those long-dead artisans was impressive, but close to it, it was breathtaking!

The place was in darkness. Conscious of a vague sense of dissatisfaction—to call it anticlimax would have been an overstatement—Marco walked in, shrugged and said to himself, 'What else did you expect, Marco? A red carpet, a band playing?'

A fresh-faced English girl in her transparent nightdress?

Pushing away the intrusive and frankly preposterous suggestion he walked past the rash of ugly builders' skips that competed with the classical statues that lined the driveway.

The oak-banded door swung inwards at a touch; inside was silence and darkness. Marco's eyes strained in the darkness as he reached behind him for the light switch. He flicked it and cursed softly when nothing happened.

Walking cautiously across to the other side of the room he found that a second switch produced a similar non-result. No electricity or a more localised fault? he wondered.

Either way his whim was looking less of a good idea by the second. Some people might make the connection with this sudden outbreak of impetuous choices and the arrival of a certain prim English girl into his life.

Marco did not.

Though a mental image of her sleeping in the old nursery where Natalia had housed her did filter through his mental barrier. It had been a long day and she was definitely a woman who would look better without clothes, though the T-shirt and jeans tightly cinched in at the waist she had been wearing the last time he'd put in an appearance had been a good look too.

That had been two days ago, but while he didn't want to cramp her style—Sophie had proved herself more than capable—he did want to be supportive, or so he told himself. What other explanation could there be for his continued visits over these past few weeks?

And it was possible that some of the men might mistake her friendliness for something else and he didn't want them getting out of line. And it wasn't just them; the young academic the museum had sent, who looked more like a surfer than a professor, had made several return visits that to Marco's mind seemed frankly unnecessary.

As he approached the sweeping staircase, at the back of his mind Marco was conscious of the fact that he would have to pass the door of the old nursery to get to his own bedroom.

As he mounted the staircase a light shining under the double doors that led into the ballroom caught his attention.

He paused and retraced his footsteps. Entering the ballroom he discovered that the vast space had not been spared the power failure; the light came from several battery-fed spotlights around the room.

His eyes lifted, and he breathed an awed, '*Dio mio,*' under his breath, for Sophie had clearly pulled off a minor miracle.

His glance moved to the scaffold tower. Something had been left on the platform. Then the something moved and he realised it was someone.

His smile faded and a strangled curse was drawn from his throat when he identified the figure lying on the gently swaying platform suspended some twenty feet above his head.

'What do you think you are you doing up there, woman?'

The question—only one person in the universe had a voice like that—drew a startled squeak from Sophie.

'You're not meant to be here!' But now that he was she realised that, subconsciously at least, this was a moment she had been anticipating with a mixture of trepidation and excite-

ment. The same confusing mixture of emotions which anticipated all his appearances.

'*You* are not meant to be *there*.' He spoke levelly, not wanting
to startle her into making any sudden movements, but the vivid
mental image he had of her landing with a dull thud on the stone
floor at his feet put an extra layer of gravel in his husky voice.

*A childhood memory surfaced, a family day out rare enough
to remain in his memory even had it not been for the disaster
that had etched it there. They had arrived at the beauty spot
complete with picnic and Marco had allowed his puppy to jump
from the car ahead of him. He had watched, laughing, as the
dog chased a bird, and stopped laughing as the pup had
followed it straight over the cliff, landing on the rocks below.*

*Climbers had retrieved the broken body, but he had never
forgotten the awful thud of impact or his father's words when
he had told him that the animal had been his responsibility—
if the puppy had been restrained, on a lead...the accident would
not have happened.*

It had been his fault.

Sophie sat up cautiously, not because she was nervous—she
had a good head for heights—but because there was not a lot of
room for manoeuvre. 'You weren't meant to arrive until the
weekend,' she added, unable to keep the reproach from her voice.

The weekend, when the worst of the debris would be cleared,
and she could awe him with her efficiency and general bril-
liance. Face it, Sophie, it just isn't going happen. You appear
to be fated to have him appear at all the worst and most embarrassing moments in your life, moments when you're wearing
jeans over pyjamas.

She had actually picked out an outfit for the weekend, not
to impress him but there was nothing wrong with a girl trying
to look her best. And she was a girl; a fact that people had been
noticing, and even though the attention might have something

to do with her being the only female under seventy around, it was soothing to her ego.

'I didn't realise I had to seek permission before I visit my home and it is just as well I didn't wait,' Marco observed grimly. 'When I said I wanted a hands-on designer I did not mean this hands-on. Get down here this instant!'

Sophie, who had ducked under the barrier the stonemasons connected their safety harnesses to while he was speaking, was already on the ladder. 'All right, give me a chance!'

She slung the comment over her shoulder as she skipped her way casually down with, it seemed to a watching Marco, not a care in the world.

When he got hold of her he would…well, his intention was to throttle her, but his intentions were sometimes hard to follow through with this woman. Actually, he was not totally sure what he would do when he got his hands on her, as he knew by now that she could throw him wildly off course with a flippant comment or an inappropriate giggle.

When her feet touched the ground he was able to expel the breath trapped in his lungs on one sibilant sigh of relief. He released the icy anxiety in the same breath and fury flamed to fill the vacuum.

On the ground Sophie turned her head; the half-formed shy smile that tugged at the corners of her mouth faded abruptly as she encountered the icy glitter in his eyes.

She'd made a major miscalculation in assuming that he was irritated, arriving home to find no electricity and organised chaos, because it wasn't irritation he saw stamped on his lean features—it was anger.

It seemed like a bit of an overreaction, though she could see that the casual observer might not get the *organised* part of the chaos unless they had it explained. Plus, Marco wasn't a casual observer; he was very attached to his ancestral home and very protective.

She could feel the waves of hostility rolling off him; he'd seen the mess and he thought she was wrecking his home. Given her talent for saying the wrong thing around him she needed to choose her words with care.

Playing for time, Sophie bent forward and shook the dust out of her hair before straightening up and beginning to bang the dust from her hands on the seat of her jeans.

She might not have been quite thorough had she known that the action had drawn his attention to the curve of her bottom.

She turned slowly around and flashed an appeasing smile which abruptly lost focus.

He was standing a lot closer than she had anticipated, close enough for her to see the dark shadow on his jaw. Despite the hour he looked incredible.

Her eyes drifted over the angles of his face; drawn to the sensuous curve of his mouth, she felt something twist hard in her stomach and thought, *Stop staring like you've never seen a man before.*

She cleared her throat and managed a weak version of her smile. 'I know it *looks* bad.'

Sophie's glance moved around the ballroom. Actually, if you discounted the dust sheets, tools and equipment, it was an improvement on the retro sixties look it had been decorated in.

'And if I'd let them have their way and sandblast everything in sight we'd be finished,' she admitted.

The macho team who had arrived had laid down their blasting equipment only when they had realised she wasn't going to be pressured. It would have been quicker but she had not been willing to risk the fabric of the building to save time.

He couldn't believe she was acting as though nothing out of the ordinary had occurred. If he hadn't come when he had, that neck of hers might be lying in a pool of blood... His big hands curled into fists at his sides as he pushed away the graphic images forming in his head.

His stormy silence did not bode well. And she wished that emerald gaze would stop boring into her. She resisted the impulse to smooth her hair again—like it would make any difference—and lifted her chin, smiled pleasantly even though he was a rude rat, and was glad she did not need his admiration to get a good night's sleep. Then again, she hadn't had a good night's sleep in quite a while, but there was absolutely no connection between her insomnia and her difficult client.

'The fact is…you've got to crack a few eggs to make an omelette.' She made a very good omelette—not as good as mum's, but… She swallowed but before she could recognise the knot in her chest as homesickness, Marco's deep scathing voice jolted her back to the here and now.

'Omelettes!' His voice was shaking with suppressed emotion. 'I do not wish to talk about eggs!'

'Look, calm down—there's no need to be cranky.'

The growling noise that issued from his clenched lips suggested her advice had fallen on deaf ears. Unable to tear her eyes from the nerve that was clenching in his lean cheek she reached for one of the spare flashlights that were stacked on an upturned box.

Marco was trying, very hard, to calm himself. He was aware that he was overreacting, but she had looked so small and delicate, and thoughts of what might have happened to her were overwhelming him. He was also exhausted by constantly fighting the almost uncontrollable urge to take her in his arms.

Sophie held the flashlight out to him with a slightly shaking hand. Was she about to be fired?

He narrowed his eyes and dragged a hand through his dark hair mussing it up so that it stood up spikily on top.

The combustible quality she had always sensed was there under his urbane facade was no longer hidden.

'Look, it's not as bad as it looks. All you need is a little imagination, Mr Speranza, and you'll see…'

His nostrils flared as he sucked in an outraged breath. 'I do not lack imagination.' His imagination was still providing an image of her broken body lying still on the marble floor. 'And do not call me Mr Speranza!' he blasted. With that explosion, his self-control snapped. 'What did you think you were doing? Have you never heard of health and safety regulations? Of common sense?'

Sophie's glance slid to the scaffold. 'Oh, you mean the tower? Oh, I've got a great head for heights!' As he continued to glower, she added hastily, 'But I won't break any regs next time, if it bothers you. I'll wait until there is someone else around and use the harness.'

'There won't be a next time.'

The remaining colour left Sophie's face. Her confidence had grown but not to the point where she could consider this possibility of losing her job with anything but total horror. 'Are you sacking me?'

'I should never have given you the contract to begin with.'

Marco watched her bite her quivering lip and fought the compelling urge to wrap her in his arms and tell her he was sorry… What was happening to him? His whole body seemed to be shaking! She was driving him to distraction. He had to end this before his irrational, apparently uncontrollable, emotions drove him to do or say something seriously stupid.

'This is not the time to discuss the situation. It's late, and we both need to sleep.' It was not the only thing he needed and the constant ache of frustration was driving him slowly out of his mind.

Sophie gave a bitter laugh. 'You think I'm going to sleep knowing you're going to sack me?'

'Do not,' he gritted, 'put words into my mouth.'

She felt a surge of relief. 'Then you're not…' She stopped as he loosed a sigh of irritation between clenched teeth. 'You're right.'

Maybe, she thought, this was sleep deprivation. With luck he would be more reasonable in the morning. 'This isn't the time...'

It wasn't the time and it never would be the time because he was too big, too male and, damn it, too *everything*...! And she was so tired and frustrated that she was having serious problems with processing what he was saying. As for reading between the lines...she'd given up. The man was just too confusing, complex and unreasonable.

And her dreams... A person could not feel responsible for their subconscious but she felt irrationally guilty and also slightly panicky at the mere possibility of him suspecting the things she dreamt about him.

He won't guess unless you tell him, Sophie. And to reveal her dreams would be a quick route to not only humiliating herself but losing her job for sure. And she was becoming increasingly convinced that he was just looking for an excuse to get rid of her, and that hurt because she was knocking herself out to impress him.

She lifted a hand to her spinning head and thought, Why else does he keep appearing at such unexpected times unless it was to catch her out?

She lowered her eyes and mumbled, 'I'm tired.'

'Why do you push yourself so hard?' he asked, looking accusingly at the dark smudges under her eyes.

'Not just me—the men have been incredible. They've done a marvellous job, haven't they?' She stopped, closed her eyes and thought, *No, I can't do this—I have to know.*

She met his eyes squarely. 'Look, you can tell me, I'm not going to break down or cry on you. Did you come here tonight to sack me?' Her glance slid to his mouth and her hands clenched at her sides.

The lines of colour etched along the crests of his chiselled cheekbones deepened as he threw up his hands in a gesture of frustrated incredulity.

Like his body language, his accent too was more noticeably Latin as he pinned her with a glittering green glare and rasped in throaty outrage, '*Sack* you? I came here tonight because I would like to…' His eyes settled on her mouth and he thought, *Kiss you*.

His jaw clenched as he battled against the impulse to follow through with the thought. This is not, he reminded himself yet again, what you came here for, Marco.

Wasn't it?

Isn't this *exactly* what you wanted?

Marco dragged a hand through his hair. He had always felt contemptuous of people who employed self-deception, and it was unpleasant to recognise suddenly that he'd been guilty of that very crime.

Five minutes in it had been obvious that despite her relative inexperience Sophie was more than capable of working without supervision; she knew exactly what she was doing, yet he had spent the past two weeks using the pretext of concerned employer to check up on her, phoning *because he liked to hear her voice*.

He took a deep breath; this had to stop. He was distracted and it was affecting his work—tonight's successful business deal should have been clinched last night.

The choice was clear; he had faced similar choices before. He had weighed the advantages of having sex with a woman he was attracted to and either he'd followed through or walked away.

This was not rocket science.

For guidance he used a few simple rules, the most important being to avoid anything that pointed in the direction of emotional fireworks, and he had become quite good at spotting women who could not separate emotion from sex.

Nothing had changed; he had weighed the pros and cons in this case. In fact, he had actually weighed them several times but each time the result was the same: becoming involved with Sophie Balfour at a sexual level was a non-starter.

And yet here he was.

'What?' she asked, folding her arms across her chest and angling a cool, clear look of defiance at his face. 'Why are you staring at me like that?' A shiver moved through her body as he carried on staring. 'What do you want to do?'

A number of replies to this question crossed Marco's mind. He voiced none but that didn't stop his body reacting to the images in his head with all the restraint of an adolescent boy in the grip of hormone overload.

Maybe he should tell her—then she'd run, which would solve his problem. Or maybe she wouldn't... The chemistry was not, he was sure, one-sided.

'Well, if you do want to sack me you'll have to say it because I'm not walking.'

He ground his teeth. Why did this woman feel the need to constantly challenge him? She was incapable of compromise; she was pig-headed... As he opened his mouth to inform her that, although not fired, she was infuriating, there was a crunching sound. A small piece of debris from the platform above, dislodged by Sophie's speedy departure, hit the ground almost at his feet. The plaster almost immediately disintegrated, spraying him liberally with powdery residue.

Sophie stepped forward and began to pat ineffectually at the front of his jacket, her efforts succeeded in grinding the dust into the expensive fabric and making her painfully aware of the hardness of his lean body; his torso had as much give as a rock face.

She took a step back, not looking at him. 'Sorry.' She was guiltily aware that she had continued to pat long after it became clear her efforts were not improving matters.

She was trying not to think about the addictive quality of the stolen moments of physical contact—my God, how pathetic does that make me—when he caught her wrist. Turning it over he looked at her dusty palm, displaying what seemed to her a bizarre fascination with her fingers and her unpolished, neatly trimmed nails.

I'm like my manicure, she thought, *not decorative but suitable to purpose, and practical.* She had often told herself that she much preferred to be useful rather than decorative and in this moment she recognised what a total sham that was!

Breathing hard, Sophie finally looked up from the brown fingers curled around her narrow bones to his face. She watched the emotions flicker across his dark face, and recalled an article she had read during her research that had said never play poker with Marco Speranza. The man has no emotions to hide; he is cold ice.

Well, the ice seemed very close to melting.

CHAPTER TEN

She had never imagined that it was possible to literally ache for someone's touch. Even when they clashed—actually collided—it seemed as if there was a connection there. Why wouldn't he stop looking at her? Did he feel something too? Was there something more to this than she'd thought?

'No! It's just physical.' It's only sex and it will go away when he does, which hopefully will be soon.

She cut short the inner dialogue because he was looking at her strangely.

'What is just physical?'

She froze, her eyes widening in horror. *Oh, my God. I said it out loud!*

His eyes narrowed and his expression became suspicious. Sophie's heart sank to somewhere below her knees. This is what you get when you let your imagination run away with you.

'You are injured?'

She expelled a shaky relieved sigh. 'No, I'm fine.' As fine as someone who is in danger of getting fantasy and reality horribly confused can be.

'The work the stonemasons do…it's incredibly physical. They're real craftsmen you know,' she babbled nervously, because of the way he was staring at her…*hungrily*? No, surely that was her imagination. 'I couldn't sleep…too much caffeine.'

Too much thinking about the meaning of life and the fact it was possible she could die a virgin, which up until recently had not seemed such a terrible thing. 'And the scaffold will be down tomorrow, so tonight was my last opportunity—'

'To put yourself in danger?'

Sophie winced at the corrosive sarcasm in his voice. 'To see the relief work up close—'

'You were utterly reckless!'

The accusation made Sophie's jaw drop; if he'd accused her of being cautious or careful or even boring she could have seen where he was coming from, but reckless!

'Me?' The image of herself as some sort of wild child made Sophie smile.

The smile made his fragile control snap. 'You find this funny?' he thundered, making her jump. 'If I had not come when I did you could have...'

Too angry at being spoken to as if she was a naughty child, Sophie failed to notice the dramatic pallor that had robbed his vibrant skin of colour.

'Why did you come?' she interrupted, folding her arms across her chest and aiming a look of simmering dislike at his face.

'I'm here...' He stopped and dragged a hand through his dark hair. 'I was working late.'

'And it seemed a good idea to drive out here at, what, two in the morning...?' She raised her brows and dug her hands in the pockets of her jeans. 'Oh, sure, that sounds *really* likely.'

He didn't even bother denying it and the tacit admission that he was checking up on her, that she didn't have his trust, hurt her on a level that was personal, not professional.

'You obviously don't trust me.'

Marco, who had trust issues of his own—could he trust his control to withstand the overwhelming desire to silence her by kissing those tormenting lips?—remained silent. To bring his mouth down...to taste...

'At least you've got the grace to look guilty.'

'I am not guilty! And I do not need to explain myself to—'

'A mere employee,' she cut in, with a laugh that hid another quite irrational stab of hurt. 'Don't worry, I'm in no danger of forgetting my position.' But she was, that was the problem.

'Just in danger of breaking your neck.'

Exasperated by his apparent fixation and exhausted by the constant effort of trying to behave normally around him, she lashed out.

'You want me to fail! You don't like me!' In the act of pacing like a caged tiger in the opposite direction he stopped dead and spun back.

And small wonder! The mortified colour flew to her cheeks. 'Not that you have to like me,' she inserted quickly. 'But,' she mused, 'most people do.'

'I'm sure they do,' he said, thinking of the faceless men who had seen through her disguise, men who had been tempted by her soft feminine curves and lush lips. He pressed his fingers to the pounding in his temples and continued to pace.

Sophie read scepticism in his taut response and snapped, 'They do—I'm *nice* Sophie.' A bitter note entered her voice as she added sarcastically, 'I'm *helpful* Sophie, and I never cause a scene, or disagree or say no, even if I don't particularly—' She stopped as she reached mid-tirade and at the shrill limit of her vocal range, a look of horror spreading across her face.

'So you say, yet you appear to have acquired the knack of scene making very easily. And, no, I don't *like* you—you make my life…' The blue iridescent sheen of unshed tears halted his outpouring and filled him with a sudden and urgent need to gather her in his arms.

Refusing to recognise the emotion swelling in his chest as tenderness he inhaled deeply and, pulling his crumpled tie from his pocket, began to loop it around his throat, in a slightly belated attempt to keep things on a business footing.

'This is my home. I think you'll find it is in my best interests that you don't fail. Or, for that matter, break your neck while you're on the payroll.'

'For goodness' sake! I'm not going to break my neck.' Do not cry, do not cry. So he didn't like you; it wasn't exactly news. 'It's totally safe.' She glanced towards the scaffold and surreptitiously brushed a tear from her cheek. 'It fully complies with every safety standard. Men work up there every day.'

'Men work up there with safety harnesses, and they know what they are doing.'

Sophie's chin went up. 'And I don't…?'

His eyes narrowed on her flushed face. 'You're only trying to start an argument because you know you're in the wrong and you can't admit it.'

There was just enough truth in this claim to make Sophie very angry. She dodged his interrogative glare and shrugged. 'I was only up there for five minutes. And don't worry, I'll sign a waver if you're concerned about me suing you.'

He muttered something under his breath and took a step forward. The action had none of the lazy grace she associated with him; the tension rolled off him in waves.

Sophie swallowed. She had seen Marco look angry before—he wasn't the most patient man on the planet and she seemed to have a knack of irritating him—but this was the first time she had seen that anger raw and naked without the veneer of urbanity.

Her eyes riveted on his lean face, she nibbled nervously on her full lower lip.

This, she thought, must be how a small fluffy animal feels caught in the headlights of an oncoming juggernaut, except even the dimmest fluffy animal wouldn't be crazy enough to admire the vehicle's paintwork!

She was stupid, but my God, he really was awesome!

He looked down at her, his eyes a green glitter through the dense mesh of his sooty lashes.

In an attempt to forestall the explosion, Sophie squeaked quickly, 'Just because you have had a bad day, don't take it out on me.'

'It just so happens I have had a very good day.'

Sophie took the silent addition *until now* as read.

He inhaled and shook his head before taking another step towards her.

Sophie, who got a neat blast of the unidentifiable tension emanating from him, took a step backwards, but he carried on advancing and then her feet were not moving backwards but forwards to meet him, until they stood toe to toe.

Now how did that happen? She pressed her hand to her chest as she struggled to catch her breath… Could a person forget how to breathe?

As his hands fell heavy on her shoulders Sophie's head automatically fell backwards, to meet his gaze. Their eyes locked and she swayed towards him, the tug that drew her so strong, so impossible to resist, that she would not have been surprised to see a cord from her chest connected to his, reeling her in.

No, that's your lust.

Ignoring the contribution of the sly voice of her subconscious she tried to break the hypnotic hold of his glittering green eyes, and failed. Did she even want to succeed?

The debate in her head was unresolved. Part of her appeared pre-programmed to lean into his hardness, and it was impossible to think at all when you were being bombarded with so much information—the heat from his body, the warm musky male smell.

The constant nagging ache she had been conscious of over the past weeks became centralised as a tightness in her chest; her breasts felt heavy and tingling.

My God, he is so beautiful, she thought, helplessly dazzled as always by the stark, pure perfection of his dark features. He was lean and hard, all bone, sinew and muscle, the essence of masculinity, and, this close, close enough to feel the warmth—no, *heat*—radiating from his skin, utterly devastatingly addictive.

Sophie's heart rate quickened to a rapid thud that vibrated through her body; things shifted and moved inside her as she struggled to break the invisible chains that held her motionless.

'I...' Something in his glittering emerald stare made her voice dry.

Marco's eyes travelled slowly up the graceful pale curve of her throat. He swallowed, the muscles in his brown throat visibly working as his passion-glazed stare stilled on her lips, the hunger roaring in his blood like a fever, his laboured breath loud in the electrically charged air that separated them.

The coruscating heat in his blood, pumping to every cell in his body, disintegrated the intellectual debate he had used to distance himself from the way Sophie Balfour had burrowed into his head, his thoughts, his mind, and now she had taken control of his body also.

She had awoken feelings that he had fought and was still fighting, because she was not the sort of woman he became involved with, though some might dispute appropriateness of the term *involved* when applied to his relationships with women.

Involvement was what he assiduously avoided. He did not do live-in lovers; he applied the same simple rules to his personal life as he did to business, and it worked.

He had allowed himself to become emotionally entangled once; he had let his heart rule his head...*he* had allowed it. He hadn't fallen into the situation; he had walked into it with his eyes open.

He had deliberately ignored the warning signs. In his book that did not make him a victim but a fool—he had *wanted* to be in love.

He had wanted to create the family he had never had.

And even though Allegra was out of his life, he was still living with the fallout from that decision, the self-contempt and shame.

Allegra had used him to further her ambitions and she had dragged his name through the mud in order to achieve her ends: humiliating him.

He had learnt his lesson; he would never put that sort of power in the hands of a woman again. Emotions were dangerous and unreliable, but God, her mouth was sweet and so were the crazy, unpredictable things she said.

Sophie Balfour refused to be neatly categorized, and no matter what heading he filed her under she continued to be a distraction.

He looked at her mouth, her lips raspberry red, and thought, No, not distraction…*obsession*, and one quite clearly it was illogical to fight.

A man always craved what he was forbidden and the forbidden fruit soon lost its appeal.

'*Dio mio!*' he rasped rawly. 'I want you.'

She stopped breathing.

The air hummed with an electric expectation; the tension that hung between them was as taut as the corded muscles that stood out in his neck.

He cupped her face between his hands, sliding his fingers into her hair to frame her face. The contact feathered along her nerve endings, making her entire body thrum with desire. Her knees sagged and she caught hold of his shirt.

'This is…not happening.'

His hand slid down her back, pulling her towards him and she didn't try and stop him. *Why aren't I doing anything? Why aren't I telling him this is not an appropriate action for an employer?*

She should never have got on first-name terms with him; it had all gone downhill from there. 'Mr Speranza,' she croaked.

He gave an incredulous gasp and lowered his head close enough for her to feel the warmth of his breath, sweet and fragrant on her skin. When he spoke, she reacted as violently to his voice, a throaty whisper, as if it was a caress.

'*Miss Balfour,*' he said, managing to inject mockery and caressing warmth into her name. 'You asked me why I came…'

Sophie, her breath coming in gusty little gasps, shook her head and said, 'You came to check up on me.'

'No, Sophie, this is why I came….' Marco made the admission as much for his own benefit as hers.

Her eyes widened with shock, then closed as her lips parted under the firm pressure of his mouth. A sigh shuddered through her body and she went as limp as a rag doll in his arms.

CHAPTER ELEVEN

'YOU kissed me,' Sophie said, not opening her eyes.

She felt the vibration of laughter in his chest, but when she forced her eyelids to lift there was no corresponding smile on his lips. His lean features were taut, the golden skin stretched tight across the strong planes of his angular face. His eyes glittered like hard emeralds as he stared at her with a driven, hungry intensity that sent a fresh tingle along her nerve endings.

'And I intend to again, *bellezza mia.*' He ran his thumb slowly up her throat, following the motion with his eyes until it reached the corner of her mouth, then he looked into her eyes. 'Do you have a problem with that?'

The throaty challenge drew a whimper from Sophie's aching throat. 'I...' Her eyes locked to his, she shook her head, totally convinced that if he didn't kiss her again she would suffer permanent physical and psychological damage. It might be too late to do anything about the psychological damage because she had clearly already lost her mind.

'No problem,' she whispered, thinking, *Unless you count the fact I might fall in a heap at your feet at any moment.*

This time there was a smile, a white wolfish smile that screamed danger.

A sensible person would, she knew, have run away from a smile like that. She clung and lifted her head, welcoming the silky invasion of his probing tongue. Hunger licked along her nerve endings, drawing a lost cry from her throat as she wound her arms around his neck and kissed him back. The hunger that had been inside her exploded like a star burst.

It was several breathless moments after his mouth lifted that she opened her eyes and admitted, 'I wondered what that would be like.'

'Now you know.'

She did and life was never quite going to be the same. She had never gone in for a lot of sexual experimentation, partly because no man had ever touched her and made her forget her name, and partly because most men she knew only wanted her sisters, and she didn't want to be the runner-up prize.

'And?' Marco prompted, running a finger across the swollen outline of her trembling mouth and looking into her half-closed eyes. Her lashes brushed her softly rounded cheeks, casting shadows across the flushed curves. He traced the feathery outline of one shadow with his fingertip before kissing her hard on the mouth.

Her eyelids squeezed closed as a moan was dragged from Sophie's chest. She sighed deeply, her fingers clenching the fabric of his shirt as he nipped softly at the pink cushiony fullness of her full lower lip.

'Do I pass, *cara*?'

'Oh, yes,' she sighed into his mouth as she gripped his hair-roughened forearms.

The kiss this time had less to do with control and more to do with hunger and desperation.

His hand tangled in her hair as he tilted her head backwards to look into her face. 'You want me.' It was not a question and it did not even cross Sophie's mind to deny it.

Little broken gasps left her lips as he ran his tongue along the tremulous curve of her upper lip.

'I want you,' she agreed.

Want but had never expected to have, like being six inches taller or having men look at her face when they spoke to her rather than her breasts.

Along with the lust that slammed through him at the admission came a less-welcome emotion—guilt. The way she looked at him, the trust, the total lack of artifice, touched a dormant sense of chivalry in him.

'You need to know something.'

The urgency pumping through his body made him blunt. 'I don't do love and commitment.' The one time he had given his heart to a woman she had ripped it out and ground it up.

He was trying to tell her it was a one-night stand and not to have any expectations.

Did he think she didn't already know that?

'What makes you think I do?' she challenged. 'I have a career and…plans…' This wasn't one of them, but now wasn't the time to think about that. 'The last thing I want is a relationship,' she promised him.

The assertion should have made him feel more comfortable, but instead Marco was conscious of a vague feeling of dissatisfaction.

'Recreational sex is all I have time for.'

He pushed a strand of silky hair from her cheek. 'Can you spare a few minutes for me in your busy five-year plan?'

'I think so,' she whispered, shivering at the feathery-light kiss he pressed to her parted lips.

'And if I need more?'

She looped her arms around his neck and pressed her body to his, gasping as she felt the rock-hard impression of his erection grind into the soft flesh of her stomach.

'You can have as much as you want. You can have anything you want.'

Lust kicked in his belly as he groaned and picked her up.

He stumbled his way out of the ballroom, up the stairs and

into her bedroom, his progress impeded not just by the objects he bumped into but by the kisses she rained on his neck. His shirt was half off before he laid her on the bed; the other half took him about two seconds.

Breathing hard he leaned over her; her face was a pale blur in the dark. 'I wanted to do this with the lights on.' He had, in the privacy of his fantasies. 'But no matter, this is still better.'

'Better than what?'

Marco smiled and, supporting her weight with one arm, he whipped her nightshirt over her head.

'Better than anything,' he said, cupping one soft quivering mound in his hand and watching it spill through his fingers. He touched his tongue to the pink tip and felt her go limp in his arms. 'You're perfect, utterly and totally perfect.'

Sophie gave a sigh of voluptuous pleasure. 'God, yes,' she groaned as he laid her back down.

She felt his hands on the belt of her jeans and lifted her hips. 'This is really happening.'

'If this is a dream, *cara*, I don't want to wake up,' he confided, sliding the denims over her hips. The pyjama shorts joined them in a heap on the floor three second later.

She opened her eyes and held out her arms, a silent invitation…longing to feel the touch of his flesh against her own.

He didn't accept the invitation. He just sat there.

Fear curled in her stomach, closing her throat. 'What's wrong?'

With a groan like a man in pain Marco shook his head and rasped, 'I can't do this!'

Her stomach still ached from the imprint of his erection; it had felt very much to her as if he could.

The rejection was so abrupt and so unexpected that for a moment all Sophie did was blink. She sat up, dragged the top cover with her, self-conscious for the first time about her nakedness. She reached out and touched his cheek, her fingertips skating lightly across the surface.

He opened his eyes but didn't look at her.

He couldn't take the risk. He was a man who had always prided himself on control, but it was shredded and liable to disintegrate totally at the slightest provocation. Sophie was a walking, breathing temptation.

Lust still pumped in a hot steady stream through his body. The sight of her mouth, her eyes and her body might just be too much. Still holding her gaze, he took her fingers and, removing them from his skin, shook his head.

'Give me a minute.' It would be more than a minute before his painful arousal would allow him to walk straight, let alone think.

Sophie, feeling physically sick, sat there shivering as tears began to slide silently down her cheeks. He saw the glisten and groaned.

'Sophie!'

Sophie flinched and pulled away from the hand he laid on her shoulder. 'It's fine…I'm fine…I understand.' Actually, she didn't understand. Why was he being this cruel?

Marco swore under his breath. 'If you are fine, you are the only one.'

'Look, I understand. You don't have sex with the help—at least, apparently not when they look like me. Don't worry, I won't tell anyone… We can pretend this never happened.'

'Enough!' Ignoring her rigidity and protest he pulled her down beside him and drew her stiff body into the shelter of his arms. '*Dio*, you are shaking,' he said, running a hand down her spine.

'So are you,' she discovered, sniffing. It made her feel slightly better, but not a lot. Her entire body ached with frustration.

'You are right, I do not have sex with the *help*. But I do…I want to with you. I will with you, but you…'

He was trying to think of a nice way of saying he didn't really fancy her. 'Don't worry, it was just…I won't take it personally…'

She heard him swear.

'You will not take it personally? Then why are you crying?'

'You forgot who I was and then you…'

'Just shut up. You are speaking rubbish.' His accent suddenly sounded very strong.

'Rubbish?'

'The disparaging comments, the pull yourself to pieces before someone else does.'

His mesmeric emerald gaze burned into her as he said softly. 'It has to stop. I do not like it.'

'All right.' At that moment she would have agreed to anything he asked just for the painful pleasure of being close to all that hard male heat…just to smell his skin, feel his touch. She ached for him in a way that she had never imagined possible. The hunger lay tight like a fist low in her belly and every individual cell in her body ached.

'I cannot have sex…'

A low sound of distress escaped her lips and he kissed her hard.

'Not because I don't want to. I swear I have never wanted anything more—you are driving me crazy.'

'Then why?'

A finger to her lips hushed her protest. 'Because I have nothing to protect you.' His brow creased into a scowl of self-condemnation as he considered his criminal stupidity.

She shook her head and looked at him through a blur of emotional tears. 'What do you mean?'

A muscle clenched beside his mouth; the frustration in his eyes made them shine like the gemstones they were so often likened to. 'I mean, you are not protected, are you?' The look of total incomprehension in her swimming cobalt-blue eyes wrenched a groan from his throat.

His apparent pain confused Sophie even more.

'I mean *protection*…you're not taking the pill.'

Comprehension dawned and the mortified colour flew to Sophie's cheeks. 'No, I'm…not.'

'And I have nothing, unless you…?'

Marco watched her blush all over—well, the bits he could see anyway.

'Sorry, no.' She was filled with shame.

She wasn't a risk taker or reckless.

How, she asked herself, *could I have not have thought about the consequences?*

When Annie had revealed her unplanned pregnancy she had secretly wondered how her otherwise highly intelligent sister had not taken precautions to avoid this situation.

Sophie had found it impossible to imagine a situation where she would take the same risk.

And now she almost had! Worst of all, it hadn't been her who had shown restraint, it had been Marco. She burned with shame.

'I want babies, but not like this.'

It was Marco's turn to feel awkward; the women in his life did not talk of babies.

'My sister has a little boy. We all love him and I know she wouldn't be without him but…'

Marco nodded in understanding. 'There is no father?'

Sophie nodded. 'I wouldn't want that.' She looked at him with glowing eyes. 'Thank you.'

Marco gave an uncomfortable shrug. 'I am no saint, but I will not do that to you.'

Being regarded in the light of a noble, self-sacrificing hero made him uncomfortable, especially when he realised how close he had come to losing control. Even now his body throbbed with the need to bury himself deep in her softness and give in to the primal urge as old as time. She was so innocent, and her eyes were still blazing with unfulfilled passion—she had so much to learn.

He took her chin between his fingers and tipped her face to his. 'I said I cannot but that doesn't mean you cannot.'

'I don't understand…I'm…'

'Let me show you, *cara,* I will enjoy that.'

'But you…'

He took her hand and kissed her fingertips one by one. 'There are many ways of bringing pleasure.'

'I don't know what you mean…'

Her response gave Marco a very poor opinion of her previous lovers. He nibbled her earlobe, making her shiver, before kissing his way to her mouth and whispering against her lips, 'Let me show you.'

Dizzy with longing she said *please* at the same moment he lowered her back onto the bed and lay down beside her. Unfolding her fingers from the cover she clutched he peeled it back, exposing her beautiful body and sending the ache in his loins up another several painful notches.

One hand on the curve of her hip he looked down at her.

Sophie, suddenly overcome by the emotion, tried to turn her head.

'No, look at me, Sophie.'

She looked at him, her face filled with a mixture of longing and fear. 'I suppose this is chemistry. Mum says that cakes and love are both about chemistry—not that this is love obviously.' He didn't join her laughter. 'I'm babbling again, aren't I?'

'You're not afraid of me, are you?'

She shook her head slowly from side to side. 'I'm afraid of the way you make me feel…not in control.'

A flicker of something moved in his eyes. 'Not being in control has much to recommend it, *cara*. Stop thinking and feel it…'

She forced her lids apart and looked at him with glazed eyes. 'Feel?' she whispered throatily.

He bent his head and, with his eyes still connected with hers, pressed his mouth to the side of her mouth. 'Feel this,' he said, sliding his fingers with seductive slowness over her ribcage before cupping one aching breast in his palm and rolling the erect tight pink peak between his thumb and finger.

Sophie gasped at the contact, moaning low as his expert caresses sent ripples of sensation through her body.

She opened her mouth to tell him she could *feel* it and she liked it when his tongue slid deep into the moist warmth of her mouth, silencing her. His fingers moved lower, sliding over the curve of her belly, his touch leaving trails of tingling fire, and he seemed intent to explore every inch of her skin.

'But tonight one of us will stay in control—me. You can relax…let me do this for you.'

'Do what?'

He smiled and kissed her, a kiss that began slow and that morphed into ravening hunger.

'What a waste,' he breathed.

She lifted her passion-glazed blue eyes to his face and shook her head.

'We could have been doing this for weeks.' His voice thickened as he added, 'You have the most beautiful body I have ever seen…' The mixture of lust and reverence in his husky comment sent a thrill through her body.

'I'm…' She stopped, her eyes squeezing closed and her voice drying as his hand moved to her other breast and he bent his head to it. The erotic caress of his tongue and mouth drew a hoarse moan from her throat.

'You're so sensitive,' he rasped, sliding down her body. The friction created by his chest hair grazing her breasts drew a deep moan from her throat.

Marco watched her writhe, gasp and bite her lip as he traced a wet path with his tongue over the silky skin of her stomach. She felt like satin, warm and soft and womanly, and the scent of her skin excited him more than he would have thought possible.

Kneeling at the bottom of the bed he took one slender foot and raised it to his mouth.

'What…?' Sophie's eyes opened and she watched, startled, as he ran his tongue over the blue-veined delicate arch of her foot.

Her head fell back and she gave a slow smile. There was clearly a lot more to erogenous zones than she had imagined.

Her eyes connected with Marco's. The shadow on his jaw accented the maleness of his beautiful face, his lean, muscle-ridged torso in the half-light gleaming dull gold.

Sophie felt her throat close up as emotions rose up inside her. She could have looked at him forever and it wouldn't be long enough.

His compelling emerald eyes still on her face, Marco hooked her foot over his shoulder and, leaning forward, slid one finger along the exposed inner aspect of her silky thigh. Then he bent his head and moved closer to her aching core.

Sophie's smile vanished as she twisted and arched, and reached for him. 'This is too…I… You can't want…' she whispered.

A muscle clenched in his cheek as he took the hands outstretched to him and moved them shockingly to the damp heat between her thighs.

'That's for me.' Sophie felt the warm breath of his whisper fan on her cheek as he moved her hands, pinioning them with one of his above her head.

He arranged himself beside her and, watching her face, put his own fingers where hers had been.

Sophie lay there, open to him, her entire body suffused by a sensual lethargy.

'Feel this,' he purred, stroking her.

Sophie moaned and pushed against his hand, the shocking eroticism of his caresses driving every other thought out of her mind.

His clever fingers drove her to the brink and drew her back twice, before he slid a finger into her and stopped as an expression of shock spread across his tense sweat-slicked features.

'*Dio mio*, how is this possible?'

Sophie did not hear his hoarse question; he had touched a place inside her and the level of pleasure went up a thousandfold. It was too much…she felt as if she would explode and then she did.

There was fire and storm and then she was safe and content

in the eye of the storm, her body still throbbing with pleasurable aftershocks.

Marco did not hold her in his arms for long. He did not trust himself—the temptation was just too great.

Sophie watched him stand. 'You're going?' You were a one-night stand—of course he's going—and he's had no fun.

He bent over her and, picking up the cover from where it had slipped, draped it over her. The sight of her body only increased the pressure pounding in his skull; primitive need pulsed through his body. He ought to be shocked that she was a virgin but he wasn't. The idea of being her first lover was incredibly and painfully arousing.

He looked at her and felt feelings he did not recognise stir. 'If I don't I might do something we both could regret. It is possibly a good thing that I did not come prepared?'

Sophie, who was already feeling guilty and selfish, supposed he was trying to make her feel better until he added, 'I could have hurt you. Why didn't you tell me?'

'It didn't come into the conversation and I wasn't sure if you'd notice and…' She stopped. 'Am I still technically a virgin or did that count as…?'

'I really don't know, but we will leave no room for doubt tomorrow.'

'You're coming back?'

'I am coming back.'

Sophie smiled.

CHAPTER TWELVE

BY TWELVE the next day there was no technicality about it: she was officially no longer a virgin.

She looked at the man beside her and ran a finger along the dappled pattern on his stomach cast by the sun streaming through the slatted blind.

'You are a very beautiful man.'

'You,' Marco retorted, 'are beyond direct for a virgin.'

'Ex-virgin,' she said smugly.

'I stand corrected.'

'I nearly fell over when I saw you.' Marco had appeared at ten-thirty; walking into a meeting she was having with a fur-niture conservator he calmly announced the meeting was over.

He had then dragged—well, maybe not dragged; she had gone willingly enough—her upstairs in full view of several in-terested painters.

'Why were you surprised I said I was coming back.'

'I assumed you meant tonight.'

'If I had waited until tonight there is a strong possibility I would have killed someone.' The comment came, if not from the heart, from an area equally important to him.

Sophie hugged herself and laughed. 'God, but I love being irresistible!' It would not last but while it did she was going to enjoy it. She wouldn't allow herself to think past the moment for fear of spoiling it.

'You are.'

She turned her head. 'What?'

'Irresistible and unforgettable.' He would definitely never forget the moment he heard her startled gasp of pleasure as he had slid into her for the first time.

She had been so silky hot and tight around him that he had had to struggle for control.

Afraid of hurting her he had tried to be gentle, but Sophie had not been afraid; she had responded with all the passion he had known she possessed, wrapping her legs around him and urging him on with frantic pleas.

'What will the men think?'

Would she be able to command their respect if they thought she was sleeping with the boss? It concerned her but not, if she was honest, enough to stop her contemplating a repeat performance with pleasure.

'They will think nothing,' Marco lied, knowing that the men would realize what had happened and it was not in his view such a bad thing. He had seen the way some of them had looked at Sophie and considering how good she looked up a ladder he could not blame them.

She looked even better in his bed.

'I have decided.'

'What have you decided?'

'We will open up the palazzo. We will have a ball to show off your work.'

Sophie regarded him doubtfully. 'I have to tell you my recent experience of balls is not that great!'

Marco pushed aside her concern with a wave of his hand. 'I have seen your organisational skills—they are second to none—and if you need any help my PA is on maternity leave but I understand from her husband that she is going a little stir-crazy. She would, I'm sure, love to lend a hand.'

'You want me to organise it?' Sophie was startled by the suggestion.

He looked bemused by the question. 'Of course.'

'What date did you have in mind?'

He gave one and she looked at him in stunned horror. 'You're not serious.'

'I have every confidence in you.'

'I'm not wonder woman. The last ball I attended I hid in the kitchen with Mia...my sister,' she added in response to his questioning look.

'You have changed.'

'And you want me to be hostess too, I suppose?'

'Who else would be hostess?'

She rolled onto her stomach, an expression of anguish twisting her soft mouth downwards. 'I'm sorry, I didn't mean to remind you of Allegra.'

His expression froze. 'You did not remind me of Allegra.' Sympathy and pity were two things he did not want, especially from Sophie. 'My marriage is not a subject I wish to discuss.'

Because it was still too painful or because he couldn't bear to hear the name of the woman he still loved?

'What about your mother—wouldn't she feel slighted if a total stranger acted as hostess?'

Sophie had only recently realised his mother was *that* Carlotta Speranza. A discovery she had made when she had waded through the albums she had discovered in one of the attic rooms.

She had realised halfway through that, though there were plenty of snaps of the photogenic actress and her husband, there were none of them as a family and only a couple of formally posed ones of Marco as a boy.

When she had mentioned this to Natalia and wondered if it

was possible some albums were missing, the older woman had said, no, that wasn't likely.

She had not come right out and said that Marco was neglected as a child but from the things she had mentioned the inference that his parents were too busy with their lives to bother about him was inescapable.

'How did Marco's father die?' Sophie had asked, studying the face of the man in the photo. How could you have a child and ignore him?

It was inexplicable to Sophie.

'You don't know.' Natalia had lowered her voice and looked around as though expecting to see people lurking in the shadows. 'He was assassinated, shot. He was dead before he reached the hospital,' she said, crossing herself.

Sophie was deeply shocked by the revelation. 'Did they ever find out who did it?'

The housekeeper shook her head.

'Poor Marco.'

'Then he went and got himself married.' Muttering under her breath she loaded Sophie's plate with more of the delicious freshly baked sponge cakes topped with jewelled candied fruit, saying sternly, 'You must eat if you wish to keep that lovely figure.'

Marco thought she had a lovely figure too. Sometimes, Sophie reflected, life was very amazing.

'My mother!' Marco looked amused by the suggestion. 'She will come and be charming if she does not have a better offer but she will not exert herself.'

'You're not close,' she probed, wondering if this part of his life was forbidden her too.

'No closer than we ever have been.'

'You never speak of your family.'

'You never speak of yours,' he countered, pressing a kiss to her throat and murmuring, 'You taste good all over.'

Sophie felt it was only polite to return the compliment so it was a little later on, after a lot of frantic kissing, that she said, 'I don't mention my family because it is so large and the relationships so convoluted, it would take a week. You, on the other hand, don't mention your family because everything with you is on a need-to-know basis. But if you want to know, my father has been married three times and my mother is the only one alive. She was his second wife. She moved back to Balfour when my stepfather was killed.'

In the act of throwing off the covers Marco slid back down into the bed and pulled her to him. 'This I didn't know.'

Sophie lay her head on his chest; the steady thud of his heartbeat made her feel safe and cherished, made her feel as if she belonged.

'How?'

'It was in Sri Lanka, an intruder. I wasn't there. Mum was taking Annie and me back to school in England when it happened. Only Kat was there and she was very young.'

'And you were so much older?'

'No, but I didn't see it.' Sophie gave a shudder. 'Kat needed a lot of TLC.'

'And your TLC?'

'I was at school.'

Something in her voice made him tilt her face up to his. 'This was not a good time for you?'

'They had a good library. I like books.' Books had been her substitute for friends.

'And everything else?'

'A nightmare. I wasn't good at anything and I was only tolerated because my sisters were popular. I missed Mum and...' She stopped and tried to pull away. 'You're not interested in this ancient history and I don't normally whinge on like this.'

'You told me because I asked and I am interested.' A thunderstruck expression settled on Marco's face as he realised he spoke the truth.

He wasn't sure what, if anything, this meant but there was a shade of unease in his eyes as he threw back the covers. Depositing Sophie, who was curled up in a ball like a small kitten, a few feet away, he got up.

'I'll email you some information on the ball, guest list and so forth.'

'I haven't said yes, yet.'

Marco paused in the act of pulling his boxers up over his slim muscular hips. 'But you will.'

'Why are you so sure?'

'Because I'm irresistible too and I will say please.'

'I'd prefer a kiss.'

Marco's eyes slid from her pink just-kissed lips to the warm swell of her magnificent breasts and he grinned. 'I think we can do better than a kiss.'

CHAPTER THIRTEEN

'PROBLEMS?' Marco asked when he walked into the study and found her frowning over a colour-coded chart.

He had come straight from the office. Actually, coming straight from the office had become something of a norm of late; he was spending most of his time at the palazzo and even working from home on occasion when there were not men with hammers knocking something down.

'Not really.' She laid down her pen and got to her feet.

But didn't rush into his arms; he noticed that and he didn't like it.

'What's wrong is that Amber rang today. She mentioned that there is a job going at Purnells—they're the biggest and most prestigious interior design firm in the country.'

'The country being England.'

She assumed an expression of cheery brightness that gave no hint of the fact her heart was breaking.

Falling in love with Marco had been inevitable. She hadn't even tried to fight it; instead she'd told herself that she could live in the here and now and leave later for another day.

Well, that *other day* had come and she was consumed by a bleak, black despair at the thought of never seeing him again.

'Where else would I be looking for a job?' Amber's call had forced her hand. 'I was wondering—it was Amber's idea—if you'd mind if I gave your name as a reference. After all, I've got a lot to thank you for. Before this I'd never even have been considered for a job like yours. You've made my career.' A few weeks ago this had been all she'd dreamed of; now the knowledge left her strangely flat. 'Always supposing,' she said, adding a downbeat note, 'that I can repeat the formula with the next client…'

'You plan to sleep with the next client?'

She recoiled as though he'd struck her.

She could think of very few things worse than getting yourself seduced by Marco Speranza and then compounding it by falling helplessly in love with the man. She stuck out her chin and said, 'Isn't that why you gave me the job?'

'No, I gave you the job because I thought you had potential.'

Not fooled by his pleasantly conversational tone, Sophie read the inexplicable anger in his body language as he stalked towards the bureau. He picked up the notebook she had left lying there.

His glittering green gaze eyes remained on the smooth youthful freshness of Sophie's face as he flicked the pages filled with her neat writing.

'Have you put it in one of your lists—"get back home and find a lover," or possibly *lovers*?'

As she contemplated a life of comparing every man with Marco and being inevitably disappointed, this angry charge struck her as particularly ironic.

What was he so mad about anyway? she wondered, directing a disgruntled scowl at Marco's lean face.

'And if I have?' Her jaw fell as she watched Marco rip her notebook very neatly into four pieces before slinging them over his shoulder. 'Try a little spontaneity,' he advised. 'I am bored with your lists.'

Sophie watched the pieces flutter to the ground and felt the heat climb into her cheeks. 'And me too, no doubt. Well, tough!' she yelled.

'Tough?' he echoed.

'Yes, I'm a Balfour…'

Marco rolled his eyes and head back and muttered an imprecation in his native tongue. 'Balfour…' He lifted his head and gritted, 'If I hear that name once more I swear…'

Eyes narrowed she cut across him. 'A Balfour does not leave a job unfinished.' She threw him a look of challenge.

'Have you any idea how different you look from that day I found you asleep in my office?'

'I had not slept for twenty-four—'

'I'm not talking about the creases in your clothes. The fact is you are the sort of woman who will always look at her best without clothes.'

The matter-of-factly voiced aside drew a choked gasp from Sophie. 'If that was meant to be a compliment…I know I'm not exactly model material—'

'A fact,' he cut back smoothly. 'You fill out clothes very nicely, though obviously,' he conceded, 'you could never be a model.'

Rub salt in the wound, why don't you? Sophie thought bitterly.

'Because people would not look at the clothes you wear— they would be looking at your body…at least, men would be.' He pinned her with an intense stare. 'Don't make any decisions about a job,' he said abruptly. 'Not until after the ball.'

'But…' She stopped and shook her head. 'All right,' she agreed. 'It's not as though I've long to wait.'

A week, to be precise.

CHAPTER FOURTEEN

THE week passed and jobs were not mentioned.

Sophie shook out the dress that had arrived by courier the day before.

She didn't know whether to bless Mia or curse her, but her sister had obviously picked up on her desperation in her last letter when she had admitted she didn't have the faintest idea what to wear for the ball, where kitchen hiding was no option.

Mia, with typical thoughtful kindness, had used her magical skill with the needle to make Sophie a dress. And what a dress! Sophie thought, running a finger down the silk of the skirt.

It oozed old-Hollywood glamour; Ginger Rogers would have been happy to float around the dance floor in a dress like this. The bold dramatic red was a statement by itself. Add the suck-you-in, push-you-up bodice and the sexy swirly skirt, and it became a very loud statement!

The note Mia had sent with it said that from her letters she thought that this was the sort of thing Sophie should be wearing.

God knows what she wrote, although the postscript of *you'll knock his socks off in this* might be a clue. It was possible she had mentioned Marco once or twice.

Leaving the dress, she went downstairs to make her last round of checks before she got dressed. As she whizzed at a trot past the ballroom, the orchestra were making discordant noises that Sophie sincerely hoped would be melodious later on.

Like her, they had to pull it all together in how many hours? She consulted the watch on her wrist and resisted the temptation to sit down and weep. Weeping would not make the team doing the lights in the garden willing to change the red bulbs she had just discovered they had wrapped around the trees beside the lake for a more tasteful white.

She was tactful and diplomatic with the lighting crew and left five minutes later confident that the lighting, at least, would be perfect—the rest, well, it was too late to worry about the rest.

She just hoped she could make it back to her room before another disaster occurred.

'Where is Miss Balfour?' The man supervising the men who were attaching arrangements of white flowers to the balustrade above the pool house turned at the sound of Marco's voice.

Before the man could open his mouth he drawled, 'No, don't tell me, she's just left?'

This had been his response the last six times he had made the same enquiry and Marco was growing increasingly irritated.

Anyone would think the woman was trying to avoid him.

'She has not been here, sir, not since earlier,' the other man said. 'But I think that might be her over there.' He nodded towards the expanse that had been a meadow until it had been transformed back into the south lawn by a team of gardeners.

Marco looked and, as he did so, noticed that the six men up ladders were staring in the same direction, staring at a running figure dressed in a T-shirt and shorts.

While he understood why they were staring—the men were only human and the T-shirt was tight—it did not improve his mood.

He caught up with Sophie before she reached the terrace.

'Oh, hello...' Sophie stopped at the sound of her name.

Hands on her hips she waited for him to catch her up; her breathlessness was only partly associated with her sprint from the pool house.

Pretending an objectivity she was about a million miles from feeling, she looked Marco up and down. When she lingered too long and felt her objectivity slipping she lifted her face to his and observed with a reproachful scowl, 'You're not dressed.'

Marco's gaze travelled up from her bare toes; the pink polish on her toenails was new, but the smooth firm creamy skin of her shapely calves and firm thighs was not. Her displaying them, however, was.

Her skin never failed to amaze and arouse him; it was satiny, smooth and soft.

'That has never been a problem for you before,' Marco observed with an earthy grin. 'And you are not dressed either. I like the shorts.'

He subjected her shapely curves to a narrow-eyed scrutiny and asked, not because he had any doubts but because he liked to see her blush, 'Are you actually wearing any underclothes?'

She blushed.

'While I have no objections, you are likely to cause an industrial accident.'

'Me?' She shook her head. 'Why?'

He studied her puzzled face, a smile playing around his lips. 'You do know you are unique.'

'Unique as in freaky or unique as in—'

'Unique as in you have a body that could stop traffic at rush hour.'

Her eyes flew wide open and a slow stain of colour spread across her skin. It was impossible to hide the glow of pleasure she felt at his words.

'Not all might think so.'

But it was only one man whose opinion she cared about and he found her sexy! Inexplicable, but who was she to argue?

'Oh, believe me, Sophie, they would.' Marco found himself unable to raise even an ironic smile at the thought. 'But let me say before I get chastised for treating you like a sex object: I want you for your mind too.'

Behind the mockery, Marco knew there was a grain of truth. Of course Sophie had a body that drove him wild and she responded to him like no other woman ever had, but it wasn't just the sex he missed when they were apart.

Her unaffected enthusiasm was exhausting and occasionally irritating but also refreshing. She had a quirky irreverent sense of humour, she blurted out the first thing that came into her head and she had a deeply annoying habit of putting a positive spin on the most disheartening situations. But none of these flaws stopped him enjoying the sound of her voice…and the way she screwed up her nose…and now she was looking at him through her lashes with an almost wistful expression that made things shift inside. He frowned. It was not a feeling he was comfortable with.

'I don't mind being *your* sex object.' For the first time in her life she felt womanly and sexy and not ashamed of her curves—that was down to Marco, who had let her see herself through his eyes, and it was an incredibly empowering experience.

Accustomed all her life to thinking of herself as an ugly duckling who would always fall short of swan-like status, it had come as nothing short of a mind-altering revelation that a man as tall and lean and utterly drop-dead gorgeous as Marco could find her sexually attractive, and his uninhibited appreciation and the pleasure he took in her body had made her feel like a woman for the first time in her life.

'Actually,' she admitted huskily, 'I quite like it.' And you too, though liking hardly covered the swelling of her heart when she looked at him.

Marco's half-smile vanished as his burning eyes connected with the shy invitation shining in her china-blue eyes.

It was only the distant—but not distant enough—yell from one workman to another that prevented him from picking her up and carrying her to his bed. Well, that and the paper in his pocket.

'*Dio mio, cara*, if you don't stop looking at me like that I will not be responsible,' he growled thickly. 'Perhaps,' he added, taking a deep breath, 'we should change the subject.' He definitely could not walk straight until his level of arousal had lowered several painful notches.

Despite the fact that she had a million things to do and several hundred of the most important people in Europe were about to descend on them, Sophie found she was painfully disappointed when he did just that.

'So what,' he asked, indicating her head gear, 'is that thing on your head?' His eyes slid to the pouting outline of her mouth. Bad move, he thought, as he was forced to ruthlessly check the surge of passion that sent a fresh pulse of pain through his groin. He was clearly going insane.

Her hand went to the scarf that covered the giant pink hair rollers. She found it some comfort that his husky voice was not quite steady and it was clear from the way he was staring hungrily at her mouth that his thoughts were not on hairstyle.

'They're hair curlers—Julia put them in to straighten my hair.'

Marco could see the obvious contradiction in this sentence but decided not to go there; instead he asked, 'Who is Julia?'

He was playing for time. Decision-making was not a struggle for him; he did not overcomplicate matters as he had a goal and he went straight for it, taking the shortest route possible to reach that desired goal.

He had a great deal of success but the occasional failure was inevitable—despite what the financial gurus suggested about his infallibility—and he chalked those up to the experience part of the learning curve of life.

He did not waver or vacillate. He made decisions and lived

with the consequences. He did not anticipate failure but neither did he fear it.

So why, when he never lost sleep over the acquisition of an airline or media company, was he unable to decide whether to make his pitch to Sophie now or later?

It wasn't as if the outcome was in doubt.

It was just the timing and she did appear pretty distracted, he thought, studying her glowing face.

The word *radiant* came into his head and at the same moment so did the image of the workmen's faces as they had watched her run across the grass and he thought, why wait?

'She is Natalia's granddaughter.'

'Who is Natalia?'

'The woman who cooked your breakfast for the past thirty years…' She stopped, intercepting the gleam in his eyes. 'You're pulling my leg.'

'It is sometimes irresistible.' Much like her lips, he mused, feeling the kick of lust again as his gaze lingered on the soft pink curve.

Sophie snorted.

'Why are you having your hair done by the cook's daughter? I said you should fly in a stylist from…' He saw the mulish belligerent expression spread across her face and extended a hand, palm up, in a gesture of mock submission. 'Fine, have it your way.' Behind her smiles and quiet manner Sophie was as stubborn as anyone he had ever met, and quietly ruthless when it came to getting her own way, which was why the project had not only been brought in under budget but ahead of time.

Observing the moment that someone realised they had been gently manoeuvred into doing it the Sophie Balfour way was amusing, except when he was on the receiving end of her tactics, and even then he did not have any strong objections. It occurred to him that a few weeks earlier he would not have viewed being wrapped around the little finger of a woman with any degree of equanimity, let alone affectionate amusement.

Sophie tugged fretfully at the hem of her T-shirt. 'Marco? You were joking about me...not wearing certain items, weren't you? You can't *really* tell, can you...?' she asked in a mortified whisper as she glanced downwards, trying to assess the level of exposure.

Marco's eyes swept downwards and made the return journey as far as her breasts. He could make out the faint shadow of her nipples.

His pupils dilated and in the space of a heartbeat he was in the grip of an insatiable, ravening hunger.

It was literally agonising not to be in a position to quench it, and the pain was not helped by a masochistic portion of his brain that provided a graphic image of her sinking her fingers into his hair as he ran his tongue across one ruched pink centre and then the other, watching them harden and hearing her catch her breath and making that throaty little groan that drove him crazy.

A woman's body had never pleased him more, or tempted him more, and the thought of another man being on the receiving end of her warmth and generosity filled him with an utter repugnance.

'You can tell.'

She shot him a killer glare and crossed her hands over her chest. 'Thanks for making me feel better.'

Marco's grin was strained. 'There is a school of thought that says, if you have it flaunt it.'

He found that he had very mixed feelings about Sophie flaunting it for people who were not him, though once their relationship was on a more formal basis he could afford to be less vigilant. Then men would think twice before trespassing and she would stop talking about leaving.

His brow puckered into a thoughtful frown. He recognised that part of the problem was that Sophie didn't have a clue what effect she had on men and she appeared genuinely oblivious to the fact that she had a body that inspired lust.

The combination made her incredibly vulnerable to prowling wolves.

That one of those wolves might be able to give her the love that she deserved was a thought that Marco suppressed before it was fully formed.

He could count the number of love matches he knew of, that lasted, on one hand. And who knows if they were as happy as they appeared? he mused cynically. Marco knew only too well how deceptive appearances could be. Until Allegra's drinking had got out of control, they had presented the picture of a devoted couple.

Marriage stood a far better chance if you went into it with your eyes open. If Sophie married him, he would make her happy, not offer her false promises and break her heart.

Sure, you're saving her from heartbreak—you're a regular hero, Marco, mocked the voice of his troubled conscience.

Sophie's voice broke through his introspective chain of thought. 'Flaunting is a great policy if you have a body like your wife!'

The drop in temperature was instantaneous and dramatic.

'I have no wife.'

Marco had always known that one day that situation would change. Continuity was important and his was an ancient name and he needed to pass on that heritage, but this did not mean that he had ever anticipated the event with any degree of pleasure.

Though naturally he would approach marriage the second time around from a very different perspective; his approach would be practical, not emotional.

His lips curled into a contemptuous smile for the romantic boy he had been.

Obviously he was not going to marry anyone he was not compatible with; common interests would be high on his list of qualities necessary in a future bride. She would need to have a certain level of sophistication to feel comfortable in his world, and of course he would not marry anyone he found physically repulsive, but he did not realistically expect mind-blowing sex.

He skimmed over the fact that Sophie Balfour bore very little resemblance to the perfect candidate, instead concentrating on the attributes that he had not previously considered essential. A peaceful life was fine but he bored easily, and Sophie was not, by any stretch of the imagination, boring!

She had brought *him* back to life, not just his home, suggested the intrusive voice in his head.

She was also incapable of deceit; admittedly that could on occasion be a pain, but honesty was rare and she was loyal. Her loyalty was sometimes misplaced but you had to admire a girl who spoke up for a father who had spent years taking her for granted, taught her none of the skills required for life outside her gilded cage and then virtually thrown her to the wolves to fend for herself.

If he had a daughter he would tell her she was capable of anything and tell her that he loved her every day of her life.

'We are not discussing Allegra.'

Sophie was not fooled by his blank expression; she knew it was to hide his pain and maybe, she speculated miserably, his secret shame because he still loved the woman who had humiliated him and stamped all over his heart. He still wrote to her. She had seen the name on a handwritten letter on his desk.

A man did not react that way to the mention of a woman he was over. This was, of course, not news to Sophie but the fresh confirmation hurt anyway.

'No.' Not speaking but thinking. Maybe he thought about her when they made love; maybe it was Allegra's beautiful vivid face he saw and not her own...

Sophie swallowed as a wave of nausea washed over her.

'Are you all right?'

'Fine,' she said, forcing a smile.

He placed a thumb under her chin and tilted her face up to his. Guilt lay heavily on his conscience. She had worked herself into the ground and he had let her.

In fact, he had done more than allow it to happen; he had engineered it, and he had known she wouldn't say no because she had something to prove, but no longer to him. He realized that no matter what Sophie Balfour thought of herself, she had more backbone and sheer guts than anyone else he knew.

He felt his anger stir at the thought of the family who had allowed her to become invisible, just because she was the quiet one.

Sophie twitched her chin from his grip. 'I'm fine,' she repeated flatly. 'I'm just… I've not stopped all day. I was in the shower when I thought I'd better check things one more time…so I had to get out of the shower which is lucky, as it happens, because for some reason the men doing the lighting had put red lights…made it look like a bordello or something…' She stopped and flashed him a questioning look. 'Sorry…I'm talking too much again, aren't I?'

'I like it when you talk too much.'

'You do?'

'*Sì*, I like your voice, though I do not always understand what you're talking about. You really do look tired.' He caught her chin again and this time Sophie did not pull back; the unexpected tenderness in his eyes nailed her to the spot and brought an emotional lump the size of a tennis ball to her throat.

He tapped her nose and said sternly, 'You need to learn to delegate more.'

'I do delegate,' she protested, wondering if the flowers had been put in his mother's suite.

'You push yourself too hard.'

No matter how hard she pushed herself she knew that she

could not compete with the sort of pressure Marco put himself under, and he appeared to thrive on it.

'That's what you pay me for.' And very soon now her job and her stay here would be at an end.

His brows twitched into a frowning line. 'I do not pay you.'

'Well, indirectly, then—you pay Amber and she pays me.'

'Not enough, I would imagine.'

'It's not slave labour, though not a lot by your standards,' she admitted.

'Or your standards. You make it sound as though we live in two different worlds.'

'My father is rich and I suppose I will be one day, but not now, and I don't have expensive tastes.'

'For a Balfour,' he inserted. 'I have been looking for you for the past hour. It was almost as if you were avoiding me.'

'I've been too busy to even think about you,' she lied. 'Anyway, what's so important that you couldn't *delegate* it?'

'I would like you to consider…'

'Could we walk while you talk?' she asked, glancing at her watch and turning towards the stone facade of the palazzo. Looking at it, she felt a little glow of satisfaction, for there was nothing unloved about its appearance now. In a few short weeks she and the team had performed a small but pleasing miracle.

In a few short weeks she had fallen in love.

'I really do need to get ready and so do you.' In white shirt and denims that clung tastefully to his snaky hips and the powerful muscles of his thighs he looked pretty good already. Actually, he never looked simply good; he always looked incredible. 'Do you mind if we duck in through the library?' she asked, nodding towards the open doors that led into the only room that had not needed her attention. 'If there's a disaster I don't want to know about it until I'm dressed.'

'You have a very negative attitude. Why assume a disaster is inevitable?'

'I could bore you with the details of the last Balfour Ball…' Sophie couldn't smile. The memory and the fallout from that night were still painfully fresh in her mind. 'Let's just say that experience leads me to believe that if anything can go wrong on these occasions it will.'

'A gloomy prediction. You should learn to have a little faith or those—' Sophie almost stumbled as his thumb flicked across the grooves above her small nose '—will be permanent.'

'Some men like the lived-in look,' she claimed untruthfully. 'And you won't be so sanguine if the press tomorrow is screaming about the Speranza family's bad blood.'

'There is very little they can say about my name that they already have not.'

There was sympathy in her eyes as her gaze brushed his profile. The world thought they knew Marco Speranza. Pages of print had been devoted to his marriage break up and acrimonious divorce. His life had been dissected, his character analysed and his face and body lusted after.

She had thought much the same as the world. She had arrived thinking Marco was the sum of the press clips in Amber's research file; she had assumed that like many people with high profiles who lived their lives in the full glare of publicity, Marco needed that limelight.

Nothing could be farther from the truth. He endured publicity and never courted it. The Marco she had come to know was intensely private, perhaps in reaction to the days when his publicity-hungry parents had paraded him in front of the clicking flashbulbs, presenting the world with an image of perfect family life before they went back to their own lives, lives that did not have a place for a child.

She felt angry when she considered what a rotten childhood he had had.

'As to what I wanted to talk to you about, I thought you might like to take a look at these when you have a spare moment.'

Sophie skipped, taking the steps two at a time, before the glanced down at the sheaf of papers he had put in her hands. 'I'll make sure Amber gets them,' she promised gravely. 'When I get back.'

'They are not for Amber.'

'Oh?'

'It's a pre-nuptial agreement.'

'You're getting married.' Sophie was amazed that she sounded normal and that she was still walking. Inside she was dead—no, not dead; dead did not hurt. She was dying slowly by painful inches.

'That is the idea.' While he had not expected her to throw herself at him, he had expected a positive response, or even a response of any sort.

'Well, wow, that's…' She stopped and inhaled. 'Surprising.'

Marco watched as she walked towards the library door. 'You had no idea?'

'Idea…' She turned slowly and looked at him, the angry colour flooding her face. 'If I'd had an *idea* do you think I'd have been sleeping with you?'

'We have got very little sleep of late.'

'You're disgusting!' she choked. He didn't even have the common decency to look ashamed, and as for telling her by giving her the pre-nuptial agreement intended for his prospective bride—poor deluded and no doubt beautiful idiot—that was one step up on dumping someone by text!

She shook her head and told herself to keep it calm, keep it dignified. 'It's nice to know that you think I'm as devoid of moral principle as you are!'

The recollection of him saying on one occasion there was never more than one woman in his life at a time came back to her and Sophie saw red. Her grasp on quiet dignity faltered as she raised her eyes to his face. The lying, cheating rat had the cheek to look bewildered.

The only thing she had asked for was exclusivity for the duration, and all the time he'd been…though God knows where he found the time or energy to sleep with his prospective bride, considering the amount of each commodity he had used up in her bed!

'Has she been out of the country? Is that it, and you needed someone to fill in…?'

'Has who been out of the country?' Marco, who had never perfected the art of discovering his inner calm, repressed the urge to kick the table. One of them had to retain a little control and it clearly was not going to be Sophie.

He had not been totally sure of her reaction to his proposal but in none of the possible outcomes he had considered had she turned on him like a spitting cat.

A beautiful spitting cat admittedly, he conceded. His ability to make any sense of what she was saying was being severely hampered by the bounce and erotic sway of her unfettered bosom.

Sophie shook her head and pressed her hands to her ears. 'Don't tell me, I don't want to know!'

'You have lost one of your earrings…' Marco said.

'Like I care!' She gulped back a sob as she threw the papers back at him. 'What am I meant to do with these?'

'What are you talking about, Sophie?'

'My God, you do believe in getting your money's worth, don't you? Designer, event organiser, sex on tap and now you want me to give you legal advice. What's wrong with your lawyers, Marco?' She shook her head and ignored the hands he stretched out to her. 'I will do my part tonight,' she told him with a sniff. 'But afterwards I'm out of here,' she yelled. She would walk back to London…crawl, if necessary.

'Who do you think this contract is for?'

It wasn't the *who* that mattered; it was the fact there was a who. 'Look, I'm in no mood for twenty questions.'

'If you stop yelling for two seconds and look—'

'I—'

'The name on that contract is yours.'

Sophie stopped dead. *'What?'*

'You.'

'Me!' The angry colour receded, leaving her paper pale. *I'm shaking...I'm dreaming.*

'Me...you...marry?' Poor grammar, Sophie. She lifted a hand to her spinning head. 'This is a proposal?'

'Yes.'

'Oh, God!'

'You are practical woman, and I know you value frank speaking as much as I do.' When it came to pointing out his myriad faults, he reflected, Sophie had no equal.

Sophie eyed him uncertainly. 'Frank speaking is good,' she admitted, talking slowly as she tried to work out where he was going with this—and he clearly was determined to go somewhere. 'But sometimes a white lie can work, or even exaggeration?'

'I would not insult your intelligence by getting down on one knee and swearing eternal love.'

'No, that would have been embarrassing,' she agreed, thinking, *how can an intelligent man be so stupid?*

He nodded. 'I want a family, but I do not want a—'

'Wife?' she suggested.

He turned his frowning regard on her. 'A marriage based on unrealistic expectations and ephemeral emotions.'

'Life is pretty damned ephemeral, Marco.'

'I find you attractive and I like you. I have no problem if you wish to work—you can start your own firm if you wish. Think about it.'

Sophie watched him walk away before she closed her eyes and shook her head.

'He likes me,' she said, and burst into tears.

CHAPTER FIFTEEN

SHE paused at the top of the stairs. She was late, but that was Marco's fault; it had taken more cold compresses than she thought to soothe her puffy tear-swollen eyes, so if he didn't like it, tough.

At the top of the sweeping staircase she caught her breath at the scene below—the glitter of diamonds, the rainbow swirl of silk, the buzz of laughter and conversation audible above the soft hum of the orchestra.

It was totally magical.

It was totally terrifying.

She lifted her chin: no hiding in the kitchen with Mia this time. She might be leaving but it would not be through the kitchen door and not before she had told Marco Speranza that she would never *like* him!

Then she saw him and the defiant sparkle faded from her eyes as she gazed with helpless longing at the tall and supremely elegant figure projecting an effortless aura of cool command that she could feel from the other side of the ballroom. Her heart had stalled. She stared hungrily, until a hissing comment from Julia made her take that first step.

Marco frowned as the diplomat he was speaking to allowed his attention to very undiplomatically stray; at about the same moment he realised that the buzz of conversation in the ballroom had significantly lowered in volume.

'Sorry,' said the man beside him when he failed to respond to an enquiry from Marco. 'But who is that incredible woman?'

Marco followed the direction of the other man's stare and his covetous gaze stilled on the figure gliding down the staircase. The figure wearing a red dress that clung lovingly to every proud curve, a figure that oozed an earthy warm sex appeal that had heads turning and jaws dropping.

She looked like a queen.

A combination of pride and lust pushed every other thought from his head as, without replying, Marco began to move forward, his eyes glued to the figure in the red dress. People parted to let him through.

He was at the foot of the staircase as Sophie reached the bottom. Without a word he held out his hand. She saw the muscles in his brown throat ripple, then their glances locked and for a moment she hesitated. Then, loosing a tiny, fractured sigh, she laid her small hand on his and he smiled.

The danger in that smile made her stomach dissolve in hot liquid excitement.

In a dream-like state Sophie allowed Marco to lead her out onto the dance floor. Her heart was pounding so hard that she could hardly breathe; walking away had seemed so easy when she was upstairs indulging her self-righteous anger but the moment their eyes connected she had known that it would take every ounce of will power she possessed and more.

The orchestra struck up a soft, dreamy number.

'I can't dance.'

'I can. Just move your feet and I will do the rest.' His eyes slid over the creamy upper slopes of her breasts. 'Where did you get that dress?' he asked in a throaty whisper.

'Mia sent it to me. She made it.'

'She has captured your personality.'

'My personality and red and…' She stopped, flushing.

'And passion. You are a very sensual woman, Sophie.'

Only with you, she thought, as she laid her head on his shoulder. Eyes closed, she melted without thinking into his hardness as their bodies swayed in time to the music.

He could dance and she could follow. Talk about the story of my life, she thought, making a token effort to escape the narcotic tug of his rampant masculinity before melting some more.

The music stopped and Sophie raised her head.

'You're a very good dancer, Marco.' He was clearly good at everything except proposals.

Marco's heavy-lidded eyes glittered emerald in his sombre tense face. 'Let's go,' he said thickly.

Sophie stared at him blankly. Was he serious? 'This is your party.'

A voice behind Sophie made Marco pull away and she heard him swear before he inclined his head and said, 'Mother, this is Sophie.'

'The clever girl who is responsible for all this?' Without waiting for a reply Carlotta Speranza took both Sophie's hands firmly in hers and drew her away. For a slight woman she could be rather forceful, but then she was a Speranza.

'There are so many people who are longing to meet you.'

'I don't think…'

The actress ignored her faltering protest. 'And your father… how is he…? We met at my last premiere…an attractive man and you have his eyes. Doesn't she, Marco? Oh, where has that man gone…?'

Sophie, who knew exactly where he was, didn't say anything. Marco was standing on the dance floor where she had left him, staring at her with a nerve-shredding intensity.

He would come and rescue her soon, she thought, and when he didn't she rescued herself from the attention of his overwhelming mother by accepting an invitation to dance from a sweet young man who said he raced cars.

When Sophie, who was calling on her rusty social skills, pretended interest in cars and asked what his real job was, he looked startled and then laughed and told her she was delicious, adding that he assumed she wasn't a fan of formula-one racing.

The conversation went on a few minutes longer before a strange idea occurred to her.

'Are you flirting with me?' she blurted unthinkingly.

'If you have to ask, not very well,' her companion replied with a grin.

'Oh, I'm no judge,' she reassured him. Her experience was limited to one man and he didn't flirt—he seduced.

Across the room Marco watched Clermont, a man almost as well known for the hearts he broke as the races he won, throw back his head and laugh before leaning into Sophie and saying something that made her blush. But she didn't, he noticed, clenching his teeth, pull away.

He did not notice the man he had been speaking with observe with alarm the murderous expression on his host's face and drift away.

His little ingénue was flirting and enjoying it.

Marco experienced a moment of chilling déjà vu. He had already married one woman who had appeared all sweetness and innocence and then watched her turn into a money-hungry tramp with all the morals of a call girl.

Was his judgement fatally flawed?

As Marco took a step forward, struggling with a level of rage he had never before experienced, Sophie, her cheeks flushed and her blue eyes sparkling, was whisked past him in the arms of an admiring middle-aged man, whose wife called a warning out to Sophie to mind her feet.

Marco, a low growl still vibrating in his throat, stopped

dead. He had been comparing Sophie to Allegra. What sort of insanity was that?

He experienced a wave of utter revulsion as he dragged an unsteady hand through his hair. How could he have thought even for one insanely jealous moment that there was a parallel between the two women?

If he let the Allegra experience poison his mind and ruin his chances of ever having a relationship that wasn't based on mutual suspicion she really would have won.

Allegra would have done anything, said anything, to be what she imagined he wanted—to get his ring on her finger. Sophie did not say what he wanted to hear or what would make her look good in his eyes; she said what was in her heart and that, he knew, was a preciously rare quality.

Allegra had used her sexuality and her body as weapons; she had been crude and coarse and vicious. Sophie was not using her sexuality to taunt him or any other man—she was discovering it and enjoying it!

And why shouldn't she?

Sophie had spent her life being overlooked by her family, had been the butt of endless family jokes, he thought, his anger against the self-obsessed Balfours momentarily submerging his self-disgust.

However, knowing that Sophie deserved the attention she was receiving did not make it easier to watch her charm the men who were drawn like moths to the flame of her warmth and glowing beauty.

It was murder, and a constant struggle, fighting the compulsion to go into full chest-beating mode and drag her away.

He resisted because he trusted Sophie, but he did not trust himself to go near her without making a total fool of himself.

Having had very little experience of being the centre of attention, it took Sophie half an hour to catch on to the fact that she was.

She wouldn't have been human if, after a lifetime of being the plain Jane in a brood of beauties, she hadn't enjoyed the novelty of the experience. But beneath the smiles and superficial gaiety she remained miserable, because the one man she wanted to tell her she was beautiful and irresistible didn't seem to want to come near her.

Having personally waved goodbye to the last VIP helicopter Sophie let her perfect hostess's smile slip and, nodding to the patrolling security guards, made her way back to the palazzo. Her path was lit by the lanterns that she had rescued weeks earlier from one of the rubbish skips.

Restored and filled with flickering flames they created exactly the ambience she had hoped for, but Sophie's thoughts were a long way from considering the pretty picture they made.

The night had been a dazzling success; she had been propositioned four times and two had come from men who were not drunk or married. And—Sophie expelled a shaky breath and felt the anger lick through her—she had also received a marriage proposal!

She had been aware of Marco watching her tonight, his brooding presence had dominated the event and her thoughts—so no change there, she thought miserably.

He had not been looking exactly happy and after that first dance and his crazy suggestion he had not come near her, though she'd caught the tail end of some of his sneery glares.

Maybe he was regretting his proposal? If you could call it that, she thought, her fists balling as she recalled his casual offhand suggestion and the contract that lay unread. On the other hand he might just be piqued because she hadn't immediately fallen over herself to accept his offer…?

And she could understand his surprise, looking at it from his point of view. She had not exactly tried to play hard to get;

she had been a total pushover, the perfect low-maintenance wife, it seemed.

She picked up her skirts and walked past the coach that was waiting for the stragglers from the orchestra, pausing to speak to the coach driver before she approached the curved sweep of stone steps that led up to the impressive entrance.

She glanced upwards; the massive double doors were flung open and the light spilled outwards, illuminating the banks of flowers that tumbled over the stone-flagged terrace onto the steps.

For a moment she felt a twinge of professional pride that almost immediately tipped over into sadness.

The problem was that this had got very personal.

This was Marco's home and she had wanted to make it a place he loved, a place where he could bring up his family. She had succeeded, and in a way that success had made her the author of her own misery.

This was Marco's retreat from the eyes of the world; it had hurt to think about him sharing it with someone, and now she had a chance to be that someone.

She had been tempted, but only for a moment.

She paused as a small laugh was drawn from her throat and she suddenly realised how much she had changed. Not so long ago she would have taken what he had offered, because she was plain, plump Sophie, who couldn't expect any more. She was Sophie, who didn't deserve the love of a man like Marco Speranza.

But now she knew that she deserved more.

She deserved a husband who loved her.

As she put her foot on the first step, three figures appeared through the double doors and paused on the veranda.

'Great—just what I need.' She took the next steps slowly.

'Here she is now.' Carlotta Speranza, the chandeliers of diamonds on her ears swinging, moved gracefully forward before Sophie had reached the top and bent forward to kiss the air either side of her cheeks. No physical contact was involved, but Sophie had already noted that physical contact was not her thing. 'Such a clever girl—you're very lucky, Marco,' she remarked, turning back to her son.

Before Sophie could reply the Speranza car pulled up on the gravel in the floodlit forecourt. The uniformed driver got out to open the passenger doors.

Sophie picked up her skirts and used the distraction it afforded to negotiate that final step and slip past them into the palazzo.

She stood for a moment framed in the doorway, the light reflecting the gold highlights in her shining hair. 'Goodnight. Excuse me, I'm a little cold.' She nodded towards the older couple and added, 'It was very nice to meet you both.' Then without waiting for a response she went inside.

Her heels clicked in the silence of the doorway; the last two musicians walked past and made their goodnights.

Then she was alone.

Sophie walked into the now-empty ballroom; the contrast with earlier was dramatic. The tables were cleared, the white linen cloths removed; the flowers destined for a local hospital had been taken away and the army of caterers had all retreated to the kitchen.

She sat down at an empty table, kicked off her shoes, stretched her toes and sniffed a flower arrangement that had presumably been deemed too wilted to make the move.

She felt pretty wilted herself, wilted and defeated. Elbows on the table she propped her chin in her hands.

You could see why he thought it was a done deal. All she'd done so far was fall in with his plans. Work for me, plan my party for me, sleep with me, fall in love with me…well, not the last. Marco had certainly not asked her to do that and, had he known, she had no doubt he would be appalled.

Marco, it seemed, was a one-woman man and he had given his heart to the gorgeous and, as far as Sophie was concerned, poisonous Allegra, and she had stamped all over it with her size sixes. Yet still when she clicked her fingers he came running.

Men were stupid, she reflected bitterly, and they wouldn't know a good woman if they fell over one—cancel that—they would run in the opposite direction if they recognised one, or marry her and look for their excitement elsewhere.

That was clearly Marco's grand plan.

Dropping her head onto the table she let out a long sibilant sigh and crossed one ankle over the other. 'Ouch!' Rubbing her shin she looked under the table to see what she'd hit herself on.

When she identified the culprit, a contemplative smile played around her lips.

'Why not?' she said, dragging out the champagne bucket that had been missed. She set it on the table and extracted the bottle from the water dotted with pieces of half-melted ice.

After a slight tussle she managed to pop the cork, sending froth all over the dress. Pressing a hand to the fizzing top she looked around for a glass, but there was none to be seen.

'Oh, well!' she said, lifting the bottle to her lips, and with a reckless, 'Cheers!' took a daring swallow.

Shaking her head as the bubbles slid down her throat she grimaced as she set the bottle back on the table. Safe, shy, hide-in-the-kitchen Sophie would never have done that, but this was the new improved version capable of being irresponsible.

'Excellent, exactly what you need, Sophie.' She took another swallow and shuddered. The new improved version didn't like the taste either, but on principle—she was hazy on what principle—she swallowed. 'Cheers to me, perfect hostess, party animal, low-maintenance wife material.'

She bit her lip on the quivering addition and the defiance died from her face.

'Tell me,' she began, directing the question around the empty ballroom.

'Tell you what?'

Sophie gasped and spun around in her seat, her knee catching the chair beside her own and sending it tumbling over.

That you love me, she thought.

Marco unpeeled himself from the wall he was leaning on and stood there, looking the epitome of what all women secretly wanted and what all men wanted to be—dark, brooding and utterly gorgeous.

And he wants to marry me! She stared at him, committing his image to memory, each proud line of his face. The knowledge that she had to walk away and never see him again lay like a lead weight in her heart.

What if I can't do it?

Sophie felt a moment of pure fear, but pushed it away and glared at him.

'Do you have to creep up like that?' she snapped, thinking maybe they could have sex one last time… That sort of thinking, Sophie, is the direction that leads to total lack of self-respect.

Marco raised a brow. 'You were too busy talking to yourself to hear me,' he observed, bending down to lift the overturned chair. Setting it upright he straddled it, his hands resting on the back.

'So your mother is gone?' she said brightly.

Marco's lips tightened. 'Finally.' For once she had been inclined to linger.

'A Balfour,' her escort had said as he got into the car. 'I couldn't be more delighted for you.'

His mother bestowed her gracious commendation. 'You have my total approval, Marco.'

The irony was not wasted on Marco, who had spent his childhood trying to gain parental approval, or at least parental attention, but had now neither wanted or needed either for many years.

'Approval for what?'

'A Balfour,' the boyfriend had said again to himself. 'Well, well, I might just drop Oscar a line. From his point of view this is very good timing. A wedding is always good press…the feel-good factor. Yes, a Balfour could be a very useful connection for you…'

Marco's hands clenched at his sides. He could contain himself no longer. It was that damned name, the same name that Sophie had been trying to live up to all her life. She'd spent all those years thinking she wasn't good enough to be a Balfour when the truth was she was too damned good!

In his opinion the Balfours needed to be given a few home truths and he would have no problem delivering them.

'Will you stop saying that!' Marco had shouted at his mother and her friend.

His mother's smile had faded, and she had cast a bewildered look towards her escort. 'Stop saying what, Marco?' Displays of emotion from her self-contained son were not something she was accustomed to.

'*Balfour!* You will not judge her on her name. No, actually,' he said, reconsidering his comment. 'You will not judge her at all. Her name is irrelevant—she is Sophie. I don't give a damn who her father is.' He drew a breath and added quietly, 'She is *herself*, which is better than I deserve.'

Having delivered this parting shot and aware that his mother was staring at him open mouthed, he had bid them both an abrupt and cold goodnight and walked away, wondering at the impulse that had made him speak out but glad he had.

Sophie was so stressed, waiting for him to speak, that she almost reached for the bottle again; the tension was unbearable—was he going to bring up the proposal or was he already having second thoughts? His enigmatic green eyes continued to move over her face; the silence stretched, the atmosphere thickened some more.

Sophie held his gaze, her sense of desperation growing with each nerve-racking second, until she could bear the silence no longer. Her lashes swept downwards and she expelled the breath trapped in her chest in a series of fractured sighs.

'So your mother enjoyed herself?' She winced, hearing the manic brightness in her tone. It was hard to tell if Marco had noticed; he looked… Abstracted was the closest she could come to describe the way he was behaving.

He shrugged with fluid grace and dragged a hand along the dark shadow on his jaw.

The action brought Sophie's eyes to the stubble. Her thoughts drifted back to…God, it was only this morning! It seemed like several lifetimes ago that she had woken in his arms determined to enjoy every second of the time they spent together, with no marriage proposals to present her with a major moral dilemma.

Only that morning he had questioned with concern the faint red marks on her breasts, suggesting, quite ludicrously, that she consult a doctor.

Then she had said, 'What a good idea, because I've nothing much to do today other than co-ordinate the caterers, arrange to increase the security at the south gate, organise the musicians transport because the coach company—'

Oblivious, it seemed, to her sarcasm he had cut across her increasingly overwrought list.

'You can delegate.'

Sophie had dropped the hand she had used to tick off the list of her tasks and stared at him, then realised where his eyes were focused and grabbed a sheet to cover her naked breasts. 'Now why didn't I think of that? I know you think you're the only one who's indispensable, but actually today I'm—'

'Calm down.'

The languid advice had made her grate her teeth.

'We can cancel, if necessary.'

'You think that's funny, I suppose?'

'I will arrange a medical consult this morning.'

That was the point where she had realised he wasn't joking and that he had suffered a sense of humour by-pass. Clearly, though he hid it well, he was feeling the pressure of the forth-coming party too, so she had explained in an embarrassed rush that he needn't worry…she didn't have anything contagious. His important guests wouldn't be contracting some rare disease.

What she had was not catching, although an epidemic of love might be interesting to observe.

'It's just your…' One hand remained clutched to the sheet pressed to her breasts as she had pointed at his face. 'Last night you hadn't shaved.'

He still hadn't, and the heavy dusting of stubble gave him a distinctly piratical air that she did not find unattractive. 'My skin is a bit sensitive.' He had been instantly contrite and promised to always shave in future.

It was then that Sophie had rather self-consciously explained that she liked the feel of his beard on her skin and it wasn't really *painful*, just…

Marco, his green eyes gleaming with wicked laughter, had let her struggle for words a while longer before he had helped her out.

'Arousing?'

The low throaty suggestion had been made in an indecently sexy voice and she had forgiven the laughter shining in his eyes because there had been other, warmer things mingled with it.

And when he had pulled the sheet from her grasp and asked how *much* she liked the feel…things from there had taken a pre-dictable course.

She had been running late and playing catch up all day because the extra hour he had suggested in bed had turned into two.

Struggling to focus on the here and now Sophie pushed away the graphic erotic images that crowded into her head and said, 'And now your mother's off to America.'

'Is she?' Marco said, sounding uninterested.

'The stage tour.' She had talked about little else all night. 'Don't you care?' She couldn't help but feel sad about the re-lationship he had with his parents.

Her family might be dysfunctional and school had been a nightmare but she had always been surrounded by love, and her heart ached for the lonely little boy Marco had been. If she ever had children she would make sure they knew they were loved and wanted and not farm them out to other people or send them to school when they were virtually babies.

'No, I don't care. Although I feel I should mention that she and her banker friend think us getting married is an excellent move. You have no idea what a weight that is off my mind.'

'You had absolutely no right to tell them we were getting married.'

'I didn't.'

Sophie ran a tongue across her dry lips and directed a suspicious glare at him. 'Then why did they act as if we...?' She stopped and directed a cranky look at him. 'Will you stop smouldering at me, it's...it's...'

'Smouldering?' he echoed, amusement briefly lightening the intensity of his stare.

'Yes, smoulder...you smoulder...'

'And you don't like it?'

Her eyes fell from the glitter in his but not before the trembling in her limbs had reached her core... *Because I do like it*, she thought, pressing a hand flat to her stomach. The pressure did nothing to ease the liquid heat deep inside.

'I can't concentrate.'

'Tell you what...I'll stop smouldering if you stop looking at me with those big blue hungry eyes.'

The eyes under discussion flew to his face. 'I do not have...' She stopped, unable to repeat the phrase which, considering the level of carnal knowledge he had of her, was faintly ludicrous.

He arched a sardonic brow. 'Why do you think my mother assumed we were an item?'

'I don't know, what have you been saying?' If he thought he could force her hand that way, he was about to learn how wrong he was. Of course, if he had chosen a persuasive route that involved touch and his mouth she would have felt a lot less secure.

'I say as little as possible to my mother. There's very little point as no subject that doesn't feature her actually gets her attention.'

An unwelcome image flashed into her head of a little boy ignored by selfish egocentric parents who were totally wrapped up in their own lives.

'It might be an idea if you told your family about us before my mother goes into networking mode.'

'Tell my…? What…?'

'The banker thinks the Balfours have useful connections and my mother has always wanted to be invited to the Balfour Ball.'

'She can have my ticket. I spent the last one in the kitchen.'

'And look at you now.'

To Sophie's dismay he accepted his own invitation, his eyes scrolling slowly upwards from her toes. By the time his glittering gaze reached her face her breathing was all over the place, but then, she thought with a spurt of resentment, he knows exactly what he can do to me and he doesn't have to even touch me to do it.

She gritted her teeth and lowered her gaze. 'It's a lovely dress. Mia has excellent taste.'

'You have an *excellent* body,' he drawled. 'And I think I like Mia better than the rest of your family.'

Sophie felt the colour mount in her cheeks and, annoyed with herself, kept her voice flat as she redirected the conversation. 'You don't know my family.' And she didn't warm to the idea of him liking Mia.

'I suppose I'll have to meet the Balfours when we're married.' And he would make it clear to them that the days of treating his wife like an extra in their exotic lives was over, he thought grimly.

Imagining the effect Marco would have on her gorgeous sisters Sophie felt queasy. As for the effect they might have on him she wasn't going there! 'You're never going to meet my family,' she told him with total confidence.

'Why, are you ashamed of me?' His glance slid to the bottle she was pushing around in circles on the table. 'Have you been drinking that?'

She slung him a look of fake defiance. 'It was a shame to let it go to waste.'

'You know you can't drink.'

It always amused him that she got giggly after one glass of wine, a refreshing change from Allegra's excesses.

The reproach drew a laugh from Sophie's aching throat. 'There were lots of things I thought I couldn't do, but I'm surprising myself every day.'

'I was going to ask, have you looked at the contract, but I can see there would be no point if you've been drinking.'

'There is no point and, for the record, Mr Moral Majority, I haven't been drinking...*yet*...' Sophie added, throwing him a look of sparkling challenge before she lifted the bottle to her lips and took a swallow.

'Elegant,' he admired.

Sophie's eyes narrowed. 'And if I want to get blind drunk I will!' she announced, fixing him with a belligerent glare. 'Actually, I'll do what I damn well please, just like you. I've no intention of reading the contract because I've no intention of marrying you.'

'*Accidenti!* You *are* drunk.'

Sophie raised a brow and thought wistfully, *I wish.* 'Let me get this straight. I must be drunk because I don't want to marry you. God, you really do love yourself, don't you!' Feeling reckless and not nearly as defiant as she wanted to be she reached for the bottle, but he moved it away. She clenched her teeth and glared at him.

'How dare you!'

'It's my champagne, *cara*. I'm only thinking of your head.' Actually, he was thinking more about other parts of her delicious body. It was hard to think about much else when she was sitting there in that dress that looked as though she had been poured into it.

A man had his limits and his libido had been wildly out of control all night, aware he had not been the only male present unable to take his eyes off her. He had been torn between the desire to pick her up and take her to bed and the strong inclination to knock the teeth of every man she had smiled at down their throats.

She had done a lot of smiling and he had totally exhausted his reserves of self-restraint. Being a modern man was exhausting.

Their combative glances locked and it was Sophie, her china-blue eyes sparkling with tears, who looked away first. She clenched her teeth, determined not to let him see her cry.

'I'll buy my own. I'll buy a crate!' She sniffed childishly.

'I do not find women who drink attractive.'

'But it's fine for men to drink.' Though Marco only did so in moderation, she had never seen him do more than toy with a glass of wine over dinner and indulge in the occasional brandy. 'You know you really are a total chauvinist!'

'Are you going to tell me any time soon what is going on?' he asked, with a sardonic smile that left his green eyes guarded. His quiet voice brought her head up. The indentation between her feathery brows deepened as she scanned his handsome face and gave a wild laugh. 'That's the worst part—you haven't the faintest idea.'

Marco's control slipped.

'Will you stop being cryptic and tell me what is wrong!'

'Do not raise your voice to me!' Actually, he had lowered his voice the way he always did when he was particularly angry.

He reached his hand toward hers as it lay on the table. 'Sophie…'

Sophie ignored the appeal in his deep voice and snatched her hand back, pretending not to notice him flinch, because she couldn't afford to allow her resolve to weaken.

'You don't have the right to yell at me. I don't work for you any more.'

'I think our relationship has moved on a little from employer–employee.'

'Employer–employee with benefits?'

Marco drummed his fingers on the table before pushing aside the chair and getting to his feet. The muscles worked in his jaw as he struggled to control his impatience.

'That was not what I meant.'

'I slept with you,' she said, making her voice hard as she tilted her head back to look up at him. 'Well, we all make mistakes, but on the plus side—'

Marco's silky voice cut across her. 'Oh, there is a plus side, then? I was beginning to wonder.'

'Tonight was a success.'

He clicked his fingers dismissively. 'To hell with tonight.'

Sophie turned her wrathful gaze on him. 'I went through hell to make this night perfect for you,' she told him in a quivering voice.

'*Perfect*,' he retorted, 'would not have included you spending the entire night flirting with every man in the room…flaunting your body,' he added, a pulse in his neck pounding as his glittering eyes raked her body.

Sophie closed her mouth. '*Flaunting!*' she echoed.

'That dress someone poured you into.' His eyes lifted from the heaving contours of her breasts and rested critically on her face. 'And that stuff on your face, it is not you.'

Not so long ago she would have been devastated by such scathing comments but though it hurt she discovered she had the confidence to lift her chin and say, 'You said you liked my dress.'

'I have changed my mind.'

'Anyway, how would you know what is me?'

'I know you better than anyone, Sophie, and I'm not just talking in the biblical sense. And I know this is not the woman I asked to marry me, or have you forgotten that? Did it slip your mind?'

Sophie lifted her shimmering eyes to his. 'I haven't forgotten.'

'And…?' he prompted, looking at her with an intensity that made her glad the table hid the fact that her knees were shaking.

'I've never been so insulted in my life.'

He paused and blinked. Twice his nostrils flared as he inhaled and pinned her with a piercing green glare. 'Some women would not consider it an insult to be asked to marry me.'

'Well, marry them, because I wouldn't marry you if you were the last man on earth!'

'Can I ask why the idea fills you with so much repugnance?'

'Because I'm *not* the *practical* woman you think I am. Just because I'm not some skinny model with legs up to her ears doesn't mean I don't have *feelings*.' Unable to repress the emotions that seethed in her chest, the declaration exploded from her. 'But most of all, I can't marry you, Marco, because I'm in love!'

'In love?'

'Yes.' Too late now to retract but she could still save herself from utter humiliation.

His classic features appeared carved of stone as he shook his dark head. 'No, you're not.'

Thrown a little by his reaction Sophie got to her feet, her actions hampered a little by her long skirts. 'Why? Aren't I *allowed* to be in love?'

'If you have some childish crush on a man…' he said, thinking he would track down this man and make very sure that he never took advantage of Sophie's trusting innocence.

Like you did?

'Not childish.'

Her eyes big and wide and impossibly blue shone with the same calm conviction that was in her voice as she said, 'And not a crush. I'll never love anyone else.' She'd never really bought into the whole soulmate thing, until she had discovered hers.

'Well, I wish you every happiness,' he snarled, aware that if he was a man with more altruism and nobility he might mean it.

'I won't be happy.' Which wouldn't make her unique. There was nothing special about her that entitled her to a happy-ever-after scenario. The world was full of unhappy people. She would blend in with life's other sad losers.

'He's in love with someone else.'

Marco rocked on his heels as though he had been struck. He shook his head in utter rejection, his hands hanging loose at his sides, clenched into white-knuckled fists as he resisted the impulse to demand the identity of this imbecile.

'No,' he said quietly. She was *his*.

They were meant to be together, did she not see this? Why had he only just realised it?

'What do you mean, *no*?'

'I mean…' He took a step towards her and caught the soft scent of her perfume, the same perfume he smelt when he buried his face in her hair and the same perfume that he smelt on his skin after she'd spent the night in his arms. Very conscious of the empty aching feeling in his chest, he said, 'Marry me. I'll make you forget him.'

She stared at him, seeing him through a blur of bitter tears and missing the extreme pallor on his face. 'If you only knew how funny that was.'

'Sophie, I…'

The sound of someone clearing his throat noisily made Marco break off and he whipped around. 'Get out!'

Sophie's opinion of the head of security went up several notches when, instead of scuttling for the door as nine out of ten men who valued their safety would have done, he nodded apologetically towards Sophie before turning to Marco.

'I'm sorry to disturb you, but…'

Marco, his body language not encouraging, gave the man a flat look from beneath heavy eyelids and said something harsh sounding in rapid Italian that Sophie couldn't have followed even had her brain not been scrambled by the heated emotional interchange. The realisation of how close she had come to blurting out that she loved him filled her with total horror.

The other man winced and replied in the same language; his conciliatory manner did not lessen the ferocious scowl on Marco's face.

'I am needed. An enterprising paparazzi has been serving canapés while snapping the guests, he would have got away with it had he not decided to help himself to some mementos on his way out.'

Marco found himself wishing that his own security had not been so thorough.

'Apparently the police were called and they want to know if I wish to press charges.'

'And do you?'

There was the glint of steel in his eyes as he responded. 'I have a reputation of guarding what is mine, *cara*.'

Sophie shivered. The underlying message was not exactly covert. 'Is that a threat?'

He smiled, revealing even white teeth and a ruthless expression. 'It is a fact.'

The calm pronouncement made far more impression than any exaggerated boast.

'Your problem is you've started believing your own press releases.'

'We will continue this discussion.'

'It's finished as far as I'm concerned.'

Eyes narrowed he took a step towards her and then stopped and threw a frustrated glance towards the exiting security chief who was speaking into an earpiece. 'I have to sort this out. Do not,' he added, pinning her with a lazer stare, 'move from that spot. I will be back directly.'

The autocratic delivery would normally have drawn a sarcastic retort from Sophie but she was just relieved that it did not even occur to him she would ignore it. If it had, she would not have put it past him to put her under guard.

She made herself wait a heart-thudding thirty seconds until his footsteps had died away before she picked up her skirts and ran as fast as her ridiculous heels would carry her.

And when they sank into the freshly watered grass of the lawn she took them off and ran barefoot over the grass. Though *stumbled* might have been a better, more accurate description as she was coping with such a tight-fitting dress.

She would weep later and think later but right now her actions were governed by instinct not logic and she had absolute tunnel vision. She had to escape. The how and where to were not a priority...the priority was getting away from Marco before her weakening resolve snapped.

Get away before she managed to rationalise a decision to say, *Yes, I'll marry you.* Before she convinced herself that she could make him love her. Before she decided that life with him on any terms was better than an existence without him—without hearing his voice, or seeing his face or smelling his skin.

Oh, my God, I need to get out of here!

Escape was a good thing but what she really needed was distance and a very thick door with locks—preferably several big ones—between them to stop her committing some ultimate act of criminal stupidity like saying, *You're the man I love!*

This was about survival.

She headed instinctively for the main gated entrance, her feet making prints in the newly watered grass. The security, she knew, was aimed at keeping people out, not keeping them in. She would pass through without comment, though the shoeless situation might cause a few raised brows.

Stopping to catch her breath, she tried to focus her thoughts. What she needed, she decided, clasping her hands to her thighs as she leaned forward panting, is sensible shoes. No...what she needed was transport. The question was what transport and how did she get it?

It was then she had her brain wave—how could she have been so slow? The air-conditioned garage complex was stuffed full of Marco's cars, and who was going to notice if one went missing?

It was not a solution that normally would have crossed her mind, but the circumstances were not normal and she was desperate.

Slipping through the trees, she passed into the courtyard where the garage was situated. Pausing to glance furtively over her shoulder she tiptoed across the cobbles. If anyone was around she'd have to think of something else…a taxi, maybe?

It was always good to have a plan B, but would a taxi come this far out at this time of night? Even if it would she doubted that it would take an IOU.

Much to her relief, nobody appeared. The courtyard area was deserted and—it got better—the folding doors of the building were half open and the lights inside were on.

There was no sound of activity so she presumed that someone had left without locking up; it was about time something went her way tonight.

The only way to find out for sure if someone was inside was to go in. Sophie took a deep breath and headed straight for the first car she saw. It happened to be a four-wheel drive and as she climbed up to the passenger seat her skirt snagged on a tool box that lay on the floor. She heard the sound of ripping fabric as she frantically pulled it free but didn't pause to look at the damage.

The key was in the ignition.

She raised her eyes and whispered a heart felt thank-you. It was as if it was meant to be.

It was destiny.

It is theft, retorted the voice in her head. The same voice asked how far she was going without money or a passport, but

Sophie ignored that too. She turned the ignition. It wasn't as if she intended to keep it, just to borrow it.

She was backing out of the driveway when in the periphery of her vision she saw a figure running down the drive towards her. Without turning her head, she knew exactly who it was. Sophie jammed her foot on the accelerator and the car shot forward in a shower of gravel.

Heart thudding, she drove at speed down the driveway, hit the bend fast, then exhaled when the lights of the palazzo vanished. She had escaped. She didn't feel any better, though. In fact, she felt worse and her head hurt from trying not to hear every stupid instinct in her body screaming *turn around and go back!*

Her powers of self-preservation needed some serious work!

As she approached the tricky second bend she braked. She braked again and nothing happened.

Her last thought before she hit the bend and everything went slightly crazy was, *I'm going to die and I didn't tell Marco I love him.*

CHAPTER SIXTEEN

MARCO reached the open garage door just as the four-wheel drive drew away, spraying gravel into the air.

He swore and stood there glaring at the receding lights, his chest heaving. He couldn't believe that she had run away from him, or rather driven away like a grand-prix racing driver.

He had never chased after a woman in his life, but he was about to now and when he caught up with her he would— Before he had an opportunity to think of a punishment dire enough to fit the crime a worried-looking mechanic in overalls appeared from inside of the garage, wiping his oily hands on a cloth.

He saw Marco and looked relieved.

Marco, who barely registered his presence, didn't slow as the agitated man began to speak. He listened to the outpouring with half an ear as, face set in rigid lines of fierce determination, he headed towards the open garage door. Tonight was not going as he had planned, but then since he had walked in and found Sophie Balfour asleep in his office nothing had gone as planned. His life was falling apart.

'I wish I'd never met her!' he growled.

Never seen that face. An image formed in his head of her face, the curve of her cheek, the soft pink generosity of her lips. She was a woman with no hard edges; she was soft and warm, except when she was berating him.

About to pull open the door of the first car he came to he stopped and turned back to the mechanic, who was speaking quickly, frantic to get his point across to his obviously disinterested boss.

'What do you mean *no brakes*?' Though the bad feeling in the pit of his stomach told him the mechanic had meant exactly what he'd said.

'There are none, no brakes. I was working on them.'

'You were working on your own car?'

'No, it's not mine,' the man hastened to assure him. 'One of the guests had trouble with it and I said I'd take a look...I only left for a moment to get a drink and...whoever has taken it is going to be in real trouble when they try and brake.'

A picture of the steep bend a few hundred yards down the drive flashed into Marco's head at the same moment as there was a loud discordant noise in the distance.

Noise, then silence.

The silence was almost worse. Marco hit the ground running, his open jacket flapping as he ran. He struggled to banish the nightmare images of twisted metal, and a broken body flashed kaleidoscope-like through his mind... She was fine.

She had to be fine. He couldn't think, he needed to focus; he needed to run, he needed to get to her.

The scene that met his eyes as he rounded the bend drew a groan from his dry throat. 'This isn't happening.' He shook his head in denial of what he was seeing.

The off-roader was just that. It had overturned and taken out several saplings with it; the fallen greenery partially blocked it from view but by the light from the headlights he could see that it was upside down.

Icy tentacles of paralysing fear spread through his body, threatening briefly to overwhelm him, but Marco pushed past it.

His first instinct was to rush straight in, but he made himself pause and assess the situation.

The off-roader's position, lying at a drunken forty-five degree angle up the steep embankment at the side of the drive, was precarious. He approached it cautiously; one false move and it would crash down the slope, causing God knows how much damage to Sophie, who had to be unconscious, or else she would surely have replied to his calls.

The smell hit Marco almost immediately; his nostrils flared. The air reeked of pungent petrol fumes. With a grimace he registered the pool of petrol forming on the road below and swore. One spark and the whole thing would go up.

'Sophie!' Marco was not a praying man but he prayed now as he worked his way around the vehicle. 'Sophie!'

His frustration mounted as he saw that the driver's side of the vehicle was jammed into the grassy embankment—the door was not accessible. Still calling her name and still getting no response he worked his way back around to the passenger side, his progress hampered by the loose ground beneath his feet that kept crumbling away.

After what felt to Marco like an age he reached the door. Dropping to his knees he called her name as he heaved his upper body through the open window.

'Sophie!' Inside the fumes were thick enough to make him cough.

He scanned the interior, dread clutching like a vice in his chest, anticipating the worst. When he saw the cab was empty and she wasn't there his initial relief was quickly followed by frustration.

Where the hell was she?

He saw the piece of torn red fabric first, fluttering in the breeze that blew in through the cracked windscreen. It was when he went to pick it up that he saw the second flash of red, a smear on the windscreen, and he froze. He reached out a hand. Unable to take his eyes off the stain on his fingers he closed his eyes.

Then he shook himself and thought, Get in gear, Marco. Sophie was injured but she was alive. He had to find her and, considering the blood and the amount of petrol sloshing around, sooner would be better than later....

As he pulled himself out of the car he heard a sound.

He stopped and, head tilted on one side, listened.

Frustrated he heard nothing but the distant call of a hunting owl. Then just as he began to slide down the slope he heard it again, but this time louder; it was a definite whimper.

Forgetting caution he slid backwards down the rest of slope and, landing gracefully on his feet, moved in the direction of the sound, still calling her name frantically.

He had gone a couple of yards when she appeared out of the shadows.

She blinked in a dazed manner when she saw him and said his name.

Light-headed with sheer relief he didn't respond, he just stared. She was a pitiful sight: her beautiful dress in shreds, her face filthy, blood oozing from what looked—much to his relief—like a superficial wound on her forehead. There was also a bruise along her cheekbone but to him she had never looked more beautiful.

He wanted to throttle her and kiss her and tell her that when she left a room it was empty and if she left him he'd be empty too... He loved her.

Saying it in his head made him feel lighter somehow. It was actually a release to finally admit it to himself.

He felt elation as emotions he had kept in cold storage broke free—elation and deep shame that he had been such a coward. Post-Allegra he had channelled his energies into work and sealed his heart off behind high walls, afraid to get hurt, afraid to make a fool of himself. Allegra had only ever been able to hurt his pride, not his heart, and maybe that was part of the reason she had been so spiteful...she knew it.

Sophie had dismantled the walls he had built brick by brick.

He had told himself that she wasn't part of his plan so he had changed the plan to fit around her, because he had always known he couldn't let her go.

'You're all right.'

'Yes, I'm fine.' As if to disprove this claim she swayed. She grabbed the steadying arm that went to her waist and held on to his forearm with both hands. 'Just a bit…'

'Alive. You're alive.' A hoarse sound left his throat as he tugged her to him, then cradling the back of her head in one hand he pressed her face into his chest. His arms closed around her and she sighed and stopped fighting her feelings. This was where she wanted to be and she felt safe, and for that moment it was enough.

'I thought—' He broke off, saying something uneven in Italian.

She had never heard that note in his voice before and he sounded so strange that she made herself pull a little back. As she tilted her head to look up she was shocked by the anguish and tension stamped on his lean face.

'I thought you were—' Unable to complete the sentence he shook his head.

'Me too, for a minute,' she admitted. 'I think I was thrown clear.' She frowned; the sequence of events was still hazy.

'Are you hurt anywhere?' She stood passively while his big hands moved over her body; his light touch was clinical but the feelings it evoked were not.

Finding no obvious signs of injury Marco relaxed fractionally. 'Does it hurt anywhere?'

'No,' she lied, thinking, *everywhere*. 'Not broken,' she joked shakily, 'just bruised.'

He didn't smile back. Her hand pressed to her head, she launched into a shaky apology. 'I'm sorry about your car.'

'It's not my car.'

'Oh?' Were Italian jails nice? 'I hadn't been drinking—I'd only had two mouthfuls of the champagne…honestly! I just pressed the brakes and nothing happened. It just kept getting faster and then it tipped over twice. I wasn't going to keep the—'

'If you mention the car again I will kill you myself and save you the bother. Come, we need to get away from here, there's petrol.'

Registering the smell for the first time Sophie nodded. 'Right, of course…' she murmured.

Marco watched as she pushed her hair back from her face with her forearm. The weary gesture and her attempt at a smile made things twist inside him.

Without a word he scooped her up into his arms and strode away from the accident scene.

Even if she'd had the inclination, she didn't have the strength to resist, so instead Sophie tucked her head under his chin and held on tight.

He carried her as though she weighed nothing and he wasn't even breathing hard.

He had put a few hundred yards between them and the car wreck when she became aware of the distant sounds of sirens. Before she could comment on it there was a hiss and then a loud explosion.

With her in his arms Marco leapt forward, throwing her to the ground and covering her body with his own while the world exploded around them—at least, it felt like that to Sophie.

She had no idea of how long they lay there but when Marco finally levered himself off her the air was filled with acrid smoke fumes, and the billowing orange flames from the exploded car lit the night sky.

Sophie rolled over. 'Your face is bleeding.'

He dismissed the cut on his cheek with a shrug. 'So is yours,' he reminded her as he tugged her to her feet.

Sophie couldn't take her eyes off the blazing vehicle. 'I could have been in there.'

Marco saw the shudder run through her body. He cupped her

chin in his hand and tilted her face up to his. A nerve clenched in his cheek and his eyes were dark and shadowed as he said, 'The point is that you are *not* in there.'

She nodded. 'I know, it's just…it makes you realise how… temporary everything is…how fragile.'

His lips twisted into a smile she didn't understand as he said, 'Not everything is temporary. Some things last forever and nothing can extinguish them, not fire…' His deep voice broke huskily, his eyes flickering towards the smouldering pile of metal as he added, 'Not anything.'

Before Sophie could respond to this cryptic utterance the first fire engine drew up, followed by a second, then a police car and an ambulance.

Blinking at the sea of flashing lights Sophie shook her head. 'Goodness, that's what I call overkill.' And an overdose of testosterone, she thought as the firefighters sprang into immediate action, applying a smothering layer of foam to the flames.

'That's what I call about time,' Marco retorted as he walked forward to meet the approaching paramedics. Even with his face streaked with smoke and mud, his clothes torn and filthy, he still stood out as the man in charge among a dozen hero types.

Though she could not hear the conversation Sophie could tell by the gestures that Marco was refusing the other man's suggestion he check out his head wound.

The conversation was brief; a moment later Marco was back at her side

'You go to the hospital in the ambulance. I will follow in the car.'

'I don't need to go to the hospital.'

A spasm of irritation crossed his lean features. 'You have a head wound, you could have concussion.'

'*You* have a head wound, *you* could have concussion, but you're driving.' She furrowed her brow in an attitude of feigned bemusement. 'Is it just me? Or—'

'Enough!' Marco's deep voice cut her sarcastic protest short. 'You will go in the ambulance—this is not open to discussion.'

'But—' Sophie's eyes flew wide and she let out a yelp as he picked her up. 'What do you think you're doing?'

He handed her to a hunky paramedic and said, 'I will see you at the hospital.'

He didn't, well, not immediately. Sophie had been poked and prodded, her wounds cleaned and her X-rays pronounced clear, by the time he appeared.

'We can go home now.'

Sophie embarrassed herself terribly and probably him by wailing she had no home and bursting into loud noisy tears.

'You're carrying me again,' she complained as he strode out of the swinging glass doors.

'You know what they say, keep your enemies close and the woman you love closer.'

Sophie stopped crying and stared at him. 'That's not what they say.' She sniffed. 'And you don't.'

He turned his head and the glow in his eyes made her heart flip. 'I do love you.'

'But…'

He slid her into the passenger seat.

'No buts,' he said, placing a finger on her lips and walking over to the driver's side.

She waited until he got in and said one word.

'Allegra.'

Marco stiffened at the name. 'This has nothing to do with Allegra.'

'It has everything to do with her. I knock myself out trying to please you and still fail!'

'You have not failed.'

Sophie ignored the interruption. '*She* humiliated you and cheated on you and you still love her.'

'Allegra…' He stopped and shook his head, a look of blank incredulity spreading across his face. 'You think *I* love *Allegra*?'

His eyes scanned her face; he opened his mouth and appeared to change his mind. Then quite suddenly he smiled. Sophie, who could find nothing to laugh at in this situation, told herself he was a callous rat and she'd had a lucky escape.

Marco felt a rush of heady relief. 'And that bothers you.' It was a statement.

'I couldn't give a damn!' she flung back, then seamlessly contradicting herself yelled, 'It bothers me that you're *stupid* and sh-shallow enough to be in love with someone who isn't good enough to…to…'

As her feelings threatened to overcome her, Sophie pressed a hand to her trembling lips and shook her head mutely before choking, 'Just because she's beautiful on the outside.'

And despite lip service what man born, she thought cynically, cared a jot if a girl had a sense of humour or a lovely personality, if she was plain or fat or had cellulite. Men went for the package and in Allegra's case that package was stunning.

'I don't give a stuff about Allegra.' Marco's lips didn't even twist into their usual grimace as he said the name. 'She is the past.' He made a slashing gesture of finality before extending his hand to Sophie.

She looked at his fingers and wanted to take them, wanted to place her hand within his and feel safe and cherished, but she knew that she would be fooling herself. The safety would be an illusion.

'The past that you have been writing to.' She saw his eyes widen and said, 'Yes, I know.'

'How?'

At least he hadn't bothered denying it. 'I saw the return address on the envelope. I waited for you to tell me…I gave you every opportunity.'

'I have been corresponding with Allegra, but we have not

been exchanging love letters. I would not touch Allegra with a barge pole—I would not risk even that. Allegra is poison.

'My marriage to her was pure hell from almost day one. She never wanted me, just what I could give her. I have been corresponding not to her direct but to her lawyers. It is Allegra who insists on writing to me personally. When she left she took some items that did not belong to her,' he explained. 'It was a loss I did not discover until recently, and I needed those items back.'

'She stole something from you.'

'Yes, she did.'

'What items?'

He reached into his jacket and withdrew a box.

'It's for you,' he said, placing it on her lap.

Sophie slid him a sideways look. Marco smiled and tilted his head encouragingly towards the box.

Sophie opened it slowly and gasped.

'They're beautiful.' The sapphire-and-diamond collar were set in antique gold, and there was a matching pair of earrings beside it. 'They look very old.'

'They date back to the Arabian invasion of Sicily,' he said, watching her face.

'So old… They're beautiful, Marco, but I couldn't possibly…'

Without a word Marco got out of the car. Sophie watched, thinking, My God, is he giving up?

I haven't even had the chance to say no and he's—

'Sophie.' Marco stood at the open door beside her.

He waited until he had her attention and dropped down on one knee.

'I said I would never insult your intelligence this way but it is my intelligence that is in question. Sophie Balfour, my own dearest angel, I swear eternal love to you and ask—no, *beg*—you to marry me and…' He stopped and lifted a hand. 'One moment, I almost forgot.'

She watched, her brain still lagging one sentence behind,

though that sentence was enough to make her heart soar, as he pulled a familiar-looking legal paper from his pocket.

'This,' he said, ripping it with slow relish into eight pieces, 'we do not need.' He flung the shredded paper over his shoulder and addressed the matter in hand.

'Please do me the very great honour of being my wife. Before you say anything, let me tell you that if you say no I will be a broken man. I might even take to drink, not that I am in any way trying to influence you.' The glimmer of humour faded from his eyes as he added huskily, 'You brought my home back to life, and my heart. If you leave me, you take it with you.'

Sophie pressed a hand to her trembling lips. 'I'm not going to say no, Marco, you know that.'

Marco raised her hand to his lips. 'Where you are concerned, *cara mia*, I do not take anything for granted. I have been such a fool and a coward.' He shook his head in disgust. 'I was afraid to feel—my emotions have been in deep freeze until you, my own personal sun, melted them.' He took her face tenderly in his hands and pressed his lips to hers.

Sophie sighed and choked tearfully, 'I love you, Marco.'

'What about this man you spoke of…you invented him?'

'He's you.'

For a smart man Marco could be very stupid sometimes. The look of shock swiftly followed by complacence on his face made Sophie laugh and plead, 'Please get back in the car, people will see you.'

'I don't care if they do. I want the world to know that you are mine.'

'And you are mine?'

Marco's expression was solemn as he placed her small hand on his heart and said, 'Always. You said tonight that life is fragile and you were right—I almost lost you…' She watched the muscles in his brown throat work as he visibly struggled to regain his composure.

Sophie leaned forward and stroked his cheek, touching a finger to the fresh wound. 'I'm not going anywhere without you,' she said lovingly. 'You know what scares me, if that reporter hadn't seen Bella and Olivia having their catfight, and Daddy hadn't decided to change his ways, I would never have met you, and I would still be hiding away at Balfour being the plain one. I never feel plain with you, Marco, you've always made me feel beautiful.'

Marco rested his forehead against Sophie's. 'This is because you *are* beautiful.'

His throaty voice sent a shiver of pleasure though her body. He kissed her closed eyelids tenderly and she sighed before lifting her swimming blue eyes to his.

'Can I really be this happy?' she asked wonderingly. 'Let's go home, Marco. I like the way that sounds, *home*…I might say it again, possibly many times.'

'Yes, it does have a good ring,' he agreed, kissing the tip of her nose. 'And, yes, let us go home. I have had enough of cars for one day. They have their uses but I require more room to express my feelings tonight.'

His wicked smile made her blush.

'I have one request: do not come naked to my bed tonight.'

'What?'

He grinned at her indignation. 'I would like to see diamonds and sapphires against your skin.'

She pretended shock but was seriously aroused by the erotic suggestion. 'You are a very bad man, Marco.'

He bent his head and kissed her hard before walking around to his side of the car. He started the ignition and turned to Sophie with a smile in his eyes that made her eyes fill.

'I will attempt to always be bad for you.'

Sophie could find no fault with this plan.

Coming Next Month

from **Harlequin Presents® EXTRA.** Available November 9, 2010.

Coming Next Month

from **Harlequin Presents®.** Available November 23, 2010.

HPCNM1110

LARGER-PRINT BOOKS!

 HARLEQUIN® *Presents*~

PASSION GUARANTEED SEDUCTION

GET 2 FREE LARGER-PRINT NOVELS PLUS 2 FREE GIFTS!

YES! Please send me 2 FREE LARGER-PRINT Harlequin Presents® novels and my 2 FREE gifts (gifts are worth about $10). After receiving them, if I don't wish to receive any more books, I can return the shipping statement marked "cancel". If I don't cancel, I will receive 6 brand-new novels every month and be billed just $4.55 per book in the U.S. or $5.24 per book in Canada. That's a saving of at least 13% off the cover price! It's quite a bargain! Shipping and handling is just 50¢ per book.* I understand that accepting the 2 free books and gifts places me under no obligation to buy anything. I can always return a shipment and cancel at any time. Even if I never buy another book, the two free books and gifts are mine to keep forever.

176/376 HDN E5NG

Name _____ (PLEASE PRINT)

Address _____ Apt. #

City _____ State/Prov. _____ Zip/Postal Code

Signature (if under 18, a parent or guardian must sign)

Mail to the **Harlequin Reader Service:**
IN U.S.A.: P.O. Box 1867, Buffalo, NY 14240-1867
IN CANADA: P.O. Box 609, Fort Erie, Ontario L2A 5X3

Not valid for current subscribers to Harlequin Presents Larger-Print books.

**Are you a subscriber to Harlequin Presents books
and want to receive the larger-print edition?
Call 1-800-873-8635 today!**

* Terms and prices subject to change without notice. Prices do not include applicable taxes. Sales tax applicable in N.Y. Canadian residents will be charged applicable provincial taxes and GST. Offer not valid in Quebec. This offer is limited to one order per household. All orders subject to approval. Credit or debit balances in a customer's account(s) may be offset by any other outstanding balance owed by or to the customer. Please allow 4 to 6 weeks for delivery. Offer available while quantities last.

Your Privacy: Harlequin Books is committed to protecting your privacy. Our Privacy Policy is available online at www.eHarlequin.com or upon request from the Reader Service. From time to time we make our lists of customers available to reputable third parties who may have a product or service of interest to you. If you would prefer we not share your name and address, please check here. ☐

Help us get it right—We strive for accurate, respectful and relevant communications. To clarify or modify your communication preferences, visit us at www.ReaderService.com/consumerschoice.

HPLP10R

*See below for a sneak peek from our classic
Harlequin® Romance® line.*

Introducing DADDY BY CHRISTMAS by Patricia Thayer.

MIA caught sight of Jarrett when he walked into the open lobby. It was hard not to notice the man. In a charcoal business suit with a crisp white shirt and striped tie covered by a dark trench coat, he looked more Wall Street than small-town Colorado.

Mia couldn't blame him for keeping his distance. He was probably tired of taking care of her.

Besides, why would a man like Jarrett McKane be interested in her? Why would he want to take on a woman expecting a baby? Yet he'd done so many things for her. He'd been there when she'd needed him most. How could she not care about a man like that?

Heart pounding in her ears, she walked up behind him. Jarrett turned to face her. "Did you get enough sleep last night?"

"Yes, thanks to you," she said, wondering if he'd thought about their kiss. Her gaze went to his mouth, then she quickly glanced away. "And thank you for not bringing up my meltdown."

Jarrett couldn't stop looking at Mia. Blue was definitely her color, bringing out the richness of her eyes.

"What meltdown?" he said, trying hard to focus on what she was saying. "You were just exhausted from lack of sleep and worried about your baby."

He couldn't help remembering how, during the night, he'd kept going in to watch her sleep. How strange was that? "I hope you got enough rest."

She nodded. "Plenty. And you're a good neighbor for

coming to my rescue."

He tensed. Neighbor? *What neighbor kisses you like I did?* "That's me, just the full-service landlord," he said, trying to keep the sarcasm out of his voice. He started to leave, but she put her hand on his arm.

"Jarrett, what I meant was you went beyond helping me." Her eyes searched his face. "I've asked far too much of you."

"Did you hear me complain?"

She shook her head. "You should. I feel like I've taken advantage."

"Like I said, I haven't minded."

"And I'm grateful for everything…"

Grasping her hand on his arm, Jarrett leaned forward. The memory of last night's kiss had him aching for another. "I didn't do it for your gratitude, Mia."

Gorgeous tycoon Jarrett McKane has never believed in Christmas—but he can't help being drawn to soon-to-be-mom Mia Saunders! Christmases past were spent alone…and now Jarrett may just have a fairy-tale ending for all his Christmases future!

*Available December 2010,
only from Harlequin® Romance®.*

HREXP1210